MW00617172

Swipe Right for a Cowboy

Swipe Right for a Cowboy

A Riverrun Ranch Romance

Karen Foley

TULE
PUBLISHING

Swipe Right for a Cowboy
Copyright © 2020 Karen Foley
Tule Publishing First Printing, March 2020

The Tule Publishing, Inc.

ALL RIGHTS RESERVED

First Publication by Tule Publishing 2020

Cover design by Lee Hyat Designs at www.LeeHyat.com

No part of this book may be used or reproduced in any manner whatsoever without written permission except in the case of brief quotations embodied in critical articles and reviews.

This is a work of fiction. Names, characters, places, and incidents are products of the author's imagination or are used fictitiously. Any resemblance to actual events, locales, organizations, or persons, living or dead, is entirely coincidental.

ISBN: 978-1-951786-15-1

Chapter One

EMMALINE CLAIBORNE GLANCED at her watch for the tenth time in as many minutes. Patience was definitely not one of her strongest virtues, and she'd been sitting at the elegant mahogany bar for more than fifteen minutes already. Her date was late and although he had no way of knowing it, she had a thing about punctuality. She might have been inclined to give him the benefit of the doubt; perhaps he'd had trouble finding the restaurant or been delayed by traffic. But he had been the one to suggest they meet at the upscale Manhattan lounge, and he'd stipulated the time they would meet, so the least he could do was arrive on time.

She hoped he wouldn't turn out to be a complete jerk. She was counting on him to be all the things he'd claimed in his online dating profile. She no longer had the time or luxury of researching and meeting another guy. Honestly, after five months of nights like this one, dating felt more like exercise than fun; she'd rather be at home in her comfortable pajamas, watching some mindless television. Pushing down her rising irritation, she took a sip of the wine she had ordered, and tried her best to look as if she wasn't being stood up.

Behind the bartender, rows of whiskey bottles stood on display on mirrored shelving, the golden liquid glowing beneath museum-quality lighting. Emma could see her face reflected in the mirrored backdrop, fractured by the amber bottles. She looked paler than usual; her eyes unnaturally bright. She'd left her dark hair loose, so that it fell in heavy waves around her shoulders.

Despite the unseasonably cold June they'd been having in New York, and the chilly rain that had begun falling earlier that day, she'd squeezed herself into a little black dress with a plunging neckline that exposed the upper swells of her generous breasts. She hadn't worn it in over a year and, even though she knew she'd put on some weight, had been dismayed by how snug the dress had become. She really needed to knock off the late-night trysts with her favorite rocky road ice cream. Thank goodness for shapewear. Even now, the vise-like grip of the elastic undergarment made it impossible to do anything except sit rigidly upright and take small sips of her wine. She just hoped the excessive display of skin would be enough to entice her date into accepting her proposal. It was daring of her, really, but she had run out of options. She'd do whatever it took to get him to agree.

The buzz of voices and laughter came from the restaurant behind her, along with the clink of glassware and cutlery, and the rich sound of piano music from the baby grand in the corner. All she'd had for breakfast was a yogurt and, thinking about tonight, she'd been too on edge to eat lunch. Now the tantalizing aroma of filet mignon made her mouth water and her stomach rumble.

In the next moment, she became aware of a subtle shift in the atmosphere of the restaurant, an undercurrent of energy that hadn't existed seconds earlier. Curious, she shifted on her upholstered bar stool and looked toward the source of the sudden interest. A man had entered the restaurant amidst a swirl of wind and sheeting rain, and now he stood just inside the doorway, scanning the interior as if searching for someone.

Emma's eyes widened.

It wasn't every day you saw a real-life cowboy in Lower Manhattan, and there was no question in Emma's mind that this guy was the real deal. She should know. She'd spent a huge chunk of her childhood in Last Stand, Texas. From the broad thrust of his shoulders beneath a shearling coat, to the tapered toes of his scuffed Western boots and the dripping wet Stetson he banged against his thigh, the man was one hundred percent, unadulterated, all-American cowboy. She could almost see the dust of a cattle drive clinging to his clothes. This guy wouldn't be caught dead in designer denim.

Her gaze lifted to his face, and for a moment, she found it hard to breathe. He had light-colored eyes, a square jaw, and cheekbones you could slice your fingers on, and even from a distance she could see streaks of gold in his short brown hair. His Western gear aside, the guy still would have stood out in a New York crowd. He was hot.

Seriously hot.

In the next instant, she realized he was staring at her with an intensity that bordered on impolite. She swiveled back around and clutched the stem of her wineglass, trying to pretend she hadn't noticed him. But in the mirrored glass over the bar she watched, riveted, as he crossed the space that separated them.

Was he really singling her out? Her heart began to knock hard behind her ribs. Oh, God, please don't let him try to hit on her now, not when her date could walk through the door at any second. The last thing she needed was for Rhys Bridges to see her with another man. She couldn't afford for the thirtysomething software mogul to get the wrong idea and call off their date. Besides, as gorgeous as this stranger was, cowboys weren't her type. She wanted more than a good ol' boy who spent his days riding fences and his nights throwing back whiskey. But even that sobering thought wasn't enough to stop her from admiring the man as he approached.

He walked with an easy, rolling, loose-limbed gait, and his eyes never left hers in the mirror. When, finally, he stood just behind her, Emma's breathing was a little uneven and her palms were moist.

"Excuse me, ma'am?"

His voice was deep and whiskey-rough, sliding over Emma's senses like a delicious caress, with just enough of a drawl to know he wasn't faking it. Any of it. This guy was an authentic Texan to his bones—she'd have staked her life on it.

Unable to ignore him, she released her wineglass and turned on her stool. His shoulders were broad beneath the shearling coat, and water had beaded on the suede, running in rivulets from his shoulders and down over the fabric. Up close, she could see stubble shadowing the man's strong jaw, and his eyes were a shade of green so light and pure they reminded her of the sea glass she'd once collected as a teenager on Nantucket Island.

And his mouth…

Emma had never seen such kissable lips on a man before. Full and pink, they were totally incongruous with the hard, chiseled planes of his face. But rather than diminishing his overall manliness, they enhanced it. Emma would have bet good money that she wasn't the first woman who had looked at him and immediately thought about all the things he could do with that luscious mouth. Sitting there, staring up at him, she felt her stomach squeeze tight in a way that had nothing to do with her shapewear. The way he looked at her made her nervous, as if he knew something about her that even she didn't know. A secret, maybe, that he hadn't yet decided to share. To regain some equilibrium, she swept him with what she hoped was an amused glance.

"What's the matter, cowboy? Lose your horse? You're a long way from the ranch."

He didn't respond to the gentle ribbing. In fact, his expression was so determinedly grim that Emma thought anything resembling a smile might cause his handsome face to crack.

"Emmaline Claiborne?"

He knew her name—her *full* name. Nobody ever called her Emmaline, except maybe her father and only when she'd annoyed him. How could this man know her name? She'd never met him before, because she definitely would have remembered a face like his.

"Who's asking?"

If anything, the cowboy's expression grew even more serious. "I'm a friend of Rhys Bridges. If I'm not mistaken, you're here to meet him."

Alarm, bright and hot, flashed through Emma. "Has something happened to him?"

"No, ma'am, he's fine." The cowboy's gaze never left hers. "But he won't be meeting you tonight, or any other night. I just figured you ought to know."

Emma frowned as suspicion replaced the initial alarm. "Did Rhys send you? Did he ask you to come here?"

The cowboy hesitated. "No, ma'am. I came because I don't hold with leaving a lady waiting in a bar without any explanation."

"So where is he, then? You apparently believe I deserve an explanation, so let's hear it."

"He had a change of heart."

Emma blinked. "That's it? He just changed his mind, out of the blue?"

"It's complicated."

"How do I know you're telling the truth?" She narrowed her eyes as she assessed him. "Maybe this is how you pick up unsuspecting women, by telling them their dates aren't going to show up, and then act like you're the Lone Ranger, riding to the rescue."

The cowboy's expression didn't change. "I'm not lying to you. I just thought you should know." He paused, and his glance flickered to the door before returning to her. "I'm going to leave now."

Was this guy for real? Emma held up one finger.

"Hold on a sec. I'm going to text Rhys right now." She picked up her phone from the bar and tapped out a message.

Where are you? And who is this cowboy? Did you send him?

"He's not going to reply." The cowboy's voice was gentle. "Just so you know."

She looked up at him, frustrated. "Why couldn't he tell me himself? He has my number. He had plenty of time to cancel without making me go to the trouble of dressing up and coming out in this weather. And you, too, for that matter."

"Like I said, it's complicated."

Emma stared at the cowboy, noting the grim resignation in his eyes and something else that looked like sympathy. But Emma didn't want this man's pity.

She wanted Rhys Bridges. She needed someone with his sophistication, charm, and power. From what she'd learned about him over the past few weeks, she suspected he wouldn't be intimidated by her father, her brothers, or her family's wealth. Best of all, he hadn't been fazed by her crazy family dynamics; her father had been married three times, and had produced five children with four different women. Emma's mother had been Wife No. 3, and she'd lasted longer than the others, at five years. But in the end, she'd divorced Emma's father and returned to her home state of New York, bringing three-year-old Emma with her.

Now, looking at the cowboy, a part of her understood

he'd had no obligation to come by the ritzy restaurant to tell her she was being stood up. He could have minded his own business and let her sit there all night, wondering what had happened to her date. What he'd done was both considerate and gentlemanly. But another part of her felt annoyed and even a little hurt by the apparent rejection. She'd been counting on this date, had been certain she and Rhys would hit it off. They'd seemed so compatible during the phone conversations they'd had, and his texts had been funny and sweet. She'd liked him, which made this so much worse. Her plans to bring Rhys to her sister's wedding and show every-one that she was *fine* were falling to pieces around her. She'd chosen Rhys Bridges because he was exactly the kind of man who would make her lying, cheating, no-good ex-boyfriend, Damon Stewart, insane with jealousy. The same ex-boyfriend who was now engaged to her little sister, and whose wedding she was obliged to suffer through in just three weeks' time.

Stifling a groan of frustration, she indicated the empty stool next to her own. "Well, since you're here, you might as well have a drink. Please. It's on me."

The cowboy hesitated, and for a second Emma thought he might refuse. Then he slid a leg over the stool and placed his wet hat on the vacant one beside him. Raising a finger, he caught the bartender's attention.

"Wild Turkey, neat." The bartender poured a generous amount into a glass, and slid it toward him. The cowboy hunkered forward and cradled the tumbler of whiskey between his hands. They were the strong, square hands of a man accustomed to hard work. Emma noted he wore no rings. Now he angled his head to look at her. "For what it's worth, I'm sorry."

Emma gave a short laugh. "Why? It's not your fault. Besides, I never even met Rhys in person, so it's not like I'm heartbroken or anything."

Rhys Bridges had been a means to an end, nothing more.

The cowboy's eyes were so intense Emma had to look away. She pretended interest in her wineglass, instead, because staring at him was doing funny things to her insides. "So what's your name, cowboy? And how do you know Rhys?"

"We've been friends since, oh, about second grade."

She did look at him then. "Really?"

Reaching over, the cowboy extended his hand. "Cort Channing."

His hand was big and warm. His palms were rough with callouses, but his grip wasn't crushing. She liked that. A little too much, apparently, since she couldn't quite bring herself to release him. A smile lifted one side of his mouth as he looked at where she clung to him.

She jerked her hand away. "What brings you to New York? I mean, we don't see too many cowboys around here."

"Well, I'm partly here to see Rhys, but mostly I'm in town for the rodeo."

Of course. It all made sense now: his clothes, his easy swagger, and even the hard ridges on the palms of his hands. She'd seen the Raw Unleashed bull rider event advertised throughout the city, on billboards and the sides of buses, but hadn't paid much attention. The annual event, held at Madison Square Garden, drew tens of thousands of spectators each year, and for three or four days, Midtown Manhattan hosted hundreds of cowboys and rodeo fans.

"Right, I've seen the ads." She gave him a bright smile, when everything in her wanted to rant against the unfairness of seeing her plans ruined. "So, you have tickets to the show! That's great."

She thought a smile quirked his mouth, but it was gone before she could be certain. "Yes, ma'am."

"Well, Cort Channing, thank you for coming by to tell me I was wasting my time waiting for Rhys." She sighed. "I seem to have a knack for picking losers."

"Maybe you should have swiped left instead of right."

"Excuse me?" Emma felt warm color seep into her face at his wry reference to swiping left on a dating app, to indicate a lack of interest in meeting the person. "You know we met through a dating app?"

"Yes, ma'am, he told me." He stared into his glass for a moment before angling his head toward her. "I checked out your profile. Pretty impressive."

"You *what*?" Emma tried to recall just what she'd put on her profile page. Her age, occupation, and some hobbies and activities she thought might appeal to a man with money and influence. She may have exaggerated, just a little, about her sailing and skiing skills. "Why would you do that?"

"I wanted to be sure I'd recognize you. Your profile says you're an artist. That's pretty cool."

"An aspiring artist, actually. I work at a gallery in Midtown," she replied, ignoring the warm rush of pleasure his words caused. She didn't add that the gallery belonged to her mother, and that her job consisted mainly of coordinating events and exhibits. She did have a degree in fine arts and worked mostly in acrylics and watercolor, although she didn't consider herself to be an artist. Not a true artist, anyway. She'd never sold any of her work. Her mother frequently pressed her to exhibit her paintings, but Emma had yet to do it.

"But you felt you needed to join a dating app in order to meet Mr. Right?"

Emma barely suppressed her snort of disdain. She was so *not* looking for Mr. Right. Her foray into the world of online dating had nothing to do with romance, and everything to do with saving her pride and dignity. But she couldn't say that to this man. She didn't want his pity.

"It's not as easy as you'd think to meet people when you work full-time, even in a city as big as New York," she finally said, which was the truth. "I won't lie. I'm disappointed about Rhys, but it's probably for the best. Any guy who would stand someone up without so much as the courtesy of a phone call isn't worth the time."

"Rhys isn't a bad guy. Trust me when I tell you he had a good reason for not showing up tonight. As for not calling to cancel first—" He shrugged. "He didn't have much of a chance. Things just happened too fast."

"But you're not going to tell me what happened." Emma watched as he picked up his whiskey and drained the last bit before setting the glass down on the bar.

"No, ma'am. That's not my story to tell." Reaching inside his shearling coat, he pulled out a wallet, withdrew three ten-dollar bills, and tossed them beside the glass.

"I told you this was my treat," Emma protested.

"Sorry, but I can't let a lady buy me a drink, especially when her opinion of men isn't all that high to begin with," he said, slanting her a rueful smile.

Emma gave him a tolerant look. "I never said that."

He picked up his hat and stood up. "You didn't need to." He paused. "But I am curious. What was it about Rhys that made you choose him? I've never been on a dating app before today, but I'm guessing there must be hundreds of guys to pick from. Why him?"

Emma moistened her lips, debating how to respond. "Rhys is handsome, polished, and successful," she finally replied. "Who wouldn't want to meet a guy like that?"

Something flickered in Cort's eyes, and his gaze moved downward in a slow, deliberate inspection, lingering for a second longer than was polite over her cleavage. "You'll want to be careful. Aside from the fact that online dating is killing the art of courtship, it can also be dangerous. There're plenty of creeps out there."

Had he really used the word *courtship*? The word conjured up images of old-fashioned romance, of wildflower bouquets, lemonade and porch swings, and chaperoned barn dances. How would it feel to have a man like Cort Channing wait for you in your parents' living room, while you finished getting ready in an upstairs bedroom? Something that felt very much like longing swept through Emma.

"Thanks for your concern," she said, "but I can take care of myself."

His expression said he didn't believe her. "Can I ask how you're getting home?"

She lifted her chin. "I won't be accepting any rides from strange cowboys, if that's what you're getting at."

"That's a damned shame," he murmured. Reaching inside his coat, he took out a small envelope and opened it, withdrawing three glossy tickets. "If you change your mind, here's where you can find me for the next three days. If you're interested, that is."

There was no mistaking the ring of challenge in his tone. Ignoring her astonished expression, he handed her the tickets. They were for the bull riding event at Madison Square Garden, one for each day, and a quick glance told her they weren't cheap. She didn't want to be rude, but there was no way she'd be caught dead at a rodeo. She had no desire to see anyone get stomped on by a raging side of beef.

"I can't accept these," she protested, pushing the tickets toward him. "I'm sure there's somebody else you'd rather take and besides, I'm not sure I can get away."

"There's no pressure," he said, and closed his hand around hers so that the tickets lay curled inside her palm. "If you do show up, great. If you don't, it's been a real pleasure meeting you, Emmaline Claiborne, even if the circumstances weren't ideal. Good night."

Emma watched as he made his way toward the door. He pushed it open and thrust his hat on before turning his collar up against the wet chill and stepping out into the night.

After he left, the glamorous bar seemed to lose some of its magic.

Emma looked at the tickets in her hand. Glossy and black, they featured an image of a bull rider being tossed into the air. The words *Raw Unleashed!* were printed across the front in bright red. There was little chance she'd take the cowboy up on his offer. She didn't want to give him the wrong idea. Aside from his obvious good looks, he was the complete opposite of everything she was looking for in a man. She could just imagine how her family would react if she brought someone like Cort Channing to her sister's wedding.

The thought gave her pause.

What if she did bring a cowboy home for the wedding? Her die-hard ranching family would be flabbergasted. It would be the last thing they'd ever expect from her. Hadn't she spent the past ten years trying to show them how sophisticated and worldly she was? How much better suited she was to Manhattan than Texas? How she was every inch her mother's daughter?

Her older brothers wouldn't be able to haze a cowboy, since they were cut from the same rawhide cloth. Even her father, the taciturn and intimidating patriarch of the Claiborne family, would have a tough time pretending he didn't approve, since he was a fifth-generation cattle rancher. More importantly, if she brought a cowboy to the wedding, none of her family could accuse her of trying to compete with her sister, who'd managed to snag herself a wealthy bestselling author of espionage novels right out from under

Emma's nose.

Emma felt a familiar ache in her chest and the hot sting of tears behind her eyelids. She had never thought of Callie as her half sister, although technically she was. They had different mothers, as did most of the Claiborne children, but Callie was the only Claiborne to be born out of wedlock. Gus Claiborne's extramarital affair with Rachel Dean had destroyed his marriage to Emma's mother, although Emma suspected the marriage had been rocky from the beginning. Gus had acknowledged Callie as his daughter and provided for her financially, but he'd refused to marry Rachel Dean. He had ended his relationship with Callie's mother the day Emma's mother discovered the affair, and walked out on him.

Emma thought she could understand some of Callie's bitterness, but why take it out on *her*? With three years between them, and Emma only able to visit the ranch during school vacations, they hadn't been close growing up. Callie had always been competitive with Emma, vying for their father's attention, but she'd never guessed just how much resentment Callie harbored against her. If she had, she never would have invited her to spend the summer with her and Damon. Looking back, she realized she'd actually felt very self-important, showing her little sister around New York City and pointing out everything she was missing by remaining in Last Stand, Texas. She hadn't realized that after she'd left for the gallery each morning, Callie had taken the opportunity to get close to Damon, who had worked out of the Manhattan apartment he and Emma shared.

Looking back, all the signs of the illicit love affair had been there, almost from the start. Emma had just been too blind to recognize them and was unprepared for the betrayal. Even now, more than a year later, she still couldn't understand how two people she'd loved could conspire to destroy her so completely. They'd assured her they hadn't planned it; it had just *happened*. But she'd been blindsided, her entire world thrown into chaos. How could her judgment have been so wrong? How could she ever trust herself—or anyone else—ever again?

Now Callie and Damon were living in Texas and getting married, and Emma had no choice but to attend the wedding or risk looking both petty and pathetic. She had seriously considered not going. Every cell in her body rebelled at the thought of watching her former lover—the man she'd believed *she* would someday marry—exchange vows with her sister. But her pride had gotten the better of her, and she had determined she *would* go. She'd be damned if she'd let them think she cared. But she had counted on bringing a date, a man to play the part of her doting boyfriend and quell the sympathetic glances and whispers she would otherwise be forced to endure. But Rhys had been a no-show, and now it looked as if she'd be returning to Last Stand alone. Unless…

She looked again at the tickets in her hand. Did she dare? Could she persuade Cort Channing to escort her to her sister's wedding in just three weeks' time? He'd seemed interested in seeing her again, but would he be interested enough to accompany her to Last Stand, Texas? She would cover all his expenses, of course. Cowboys probably lived paycheck to paycheck, and she had plenty of money in her bank account for airfare, and even a new suit if he needed one, although she suspected he would be too proud to accept anything from her.

She told herself her sudden interest in Cort Channing as a potential escort had nothing to do with his beautiful eyes, or his tempting mouth, or his strong, capable-looking hands. She simply needed a date to save face, and she was running out of time.

But as she tucked the tickets back into her purse and collected her coat from the hostess, Emma knew she was lying to herself.

Chapter Two

THE NOISE LEVEL in the arena was deafening. Led Zeppelin blasted over the speakers and the roar of the crowd reverberated through the rafters of the enormous venue.

Cort didn't notice.

He was too busy trying to stay seated on the bull he'd drawn, and they hadn't even left the chute yet. The animal, a 1,900-pound Brahma bull named Hammer and Anvil, had earned a hellacious reputation in the professional bull riding community as being rank, or especially difficult to ride. In his last thirty rounds, the enormous, muscle-ripped monster had managed to buck off every bull rider in less than four seconds. Right now, he was intent on letting Cort know just how unhappy he was to have the cowboy straddling his back. Each time Cort tried to secure his riding hand, the beast would press him into the railings of the chute, or throw his head back in an attempt to unseat him—or knock him unconscious.

"Sonofabitch," Cort muttered as the infuriated animal crowded him against the steel rails once more, forcing him to grab on to the top rail and lift his leg out of the way in order to avoid having it crushed. The smell of manure and dirt and bovine sweat permeated the air.

As soon as he could, he used his free hand to work the gloved fingers of his riding hand beneath the handle of the bull rope—the flat, braided length of rope that wrapped around the bull's body just behind his front legs—and then wrapped the loose end tightly around his palm. The only thing that prevented the strap from coming loose—and launching Cort from the bull's back—was his firm grip on it. Despite the fact he'd drawn a rank bull, he felt good about this next ride. With his penchant for spinning hard and bucking high, Hammer and Anvil would earn his share of points. The tougher the bull, the higher the total score. If he could stick for eight seconds, Cort had a good chance of making it to the next round.

He'd drawn a more predictable bull for the opening go-round the previous night, and had managed to stick for the full eight seconds. He'd earned a decent, if not stellar, score. But he hadn't been injured, and that was a win, as far as he was concerned. But in order to advance to the third and final round, he needed to do better tonight. He needed to stick to this nightmare of a bull for eight seconds. Anything less would be a fail.

"Good to go?" Three cowboys stood on the back rails of the bull chute, leaning in to adjust the bull's flank strap as Cort pulled the rope tight and wrapped it one more time around his hand before laying the tail end of the rope over the handle. Lane Barlow, a good friend and fellow competitor, gave him an encouraging nod. "You watch how you dismount. This one likes to spin hard, and drop riders into the well."

Cort gave a curt nod of acknowledgment, and heard the event announcer introduce him to the crowd, before going on to describe Hammer and Anvil as a bull with an attitude, who hadn't allowed a qualified ride in the last thirty attempts. As if to emphasize that fact, the bull tossed his head, clattering his curved horns against the steel rails and causing the assembled cowboys to draw quickly back. Cort drew a deep breath. With one hand on the top rail of the chute, and the other gripping the bull rope, he gave a curt nod to the man who hung on to a rope tied to the chute's gate. In the next instant, the gate swung open and the bull exploded out of the enclosure, kicking his back legs high over his head and jerking Cort so hard, he was sure his spine had been snapped in two. And then there was nothing but the hulking, bucking, pinwheeling brute between his spurs, spinning hard as it twisted and kicked sideways.

Cort felt the strain in his back and shoulder as the bull spun away from his hand, trying furiously to dislodge him. The animal's head snapped back, and Cort only just avoided colliding with the thick, curved horns that swung like baseball bats mere inches from his face. He battled the g-forces, fighting to find his center and maintain his balance. Twice, he felt himself in danger of lifting away from the animal's back, and twice he dug his heels in and hung on. The arena was nothing more than a blur of color in his periphery as the bull whipped him around, first in one direction, and then the other, as Cort pushed deep and tightened his core. Then, like a miracle, he heard the eight-second buzzer sound. He released the bull rope and used the momentum of the bull's next kick to launch himself away from the animal. Even so, he felt a hard punch to the back of his thigh that drove him forward into the dirt. He scrambled away as two bullfighters ran in, putting themselves between Cort and the bull and distracting the animal until it gave a final snort of disdain and trotted toward the chutes.

Cort picked himself up, jubilant. Pain lashed through his leg, but he barely noticed. He'd done it. He'd conquered Hammer and Anvil, a bull described as unrideable. Grinning, he punched a fist into the air, hearing the crowd roar its approval as the announcer provided a colorful commentary. One of the bullfighters jogged over to him and returned his hat, which he'd lost during the first seconds of the round.

"Nice job." The bullfighter grinned and slapped him on the back.

Cort swiped an arm across his face and turned his attention to the scoreboard. When he saw the final score, he gave a shout and thrust his hat triumphantly into the air. It was a 92, as near to perfect as he'd ever hoped to achieve, and on a bull that better riders than him had tried—and failed—to stay on for the full eight seconds. He watched in stunned disbelief as his name ticked its way toward the top of the competition board.

He'd done it.

He'd secured a spot for the third and final go-round. Exhilaration coursed through him, dampened by the swift realization that his grandfather wasn't alive to see it, although he doubted his recent success in the arena would have changed the old man's attitude toward him. In his heyday, Hank Walker had been one of the country's top breeders of bucking bulls. Everything Cort had learned about bull riding, he'd learned on his grandfather's ranch in Bandera, Texas.

Grit.

Determination.

Blood and sweat.

Cort had given it all. But none of that had mattered, because Cort's birth father, Roy Channing, had been a swindler and a schmoozer, and after he'd conned Hank's only daughter into marrying him, he'd destroyed the old man's livelihood. He'd stolen money from the Walker safe, along with three nitrogen canisters of prized stud seed, before taking off for parts unknown, leaving behind his two-year-old son and a heartbroken wife.

But that hadn't even been the worst of it. Cort had been nine years old when he'd finally learned the truth of what his father had done, and the burden had seemed almost too much to bear. He had spent his whole life trying to atone for his father's sins, and while he understood his grandfather's bitterness, he'd never understood why that resentment and hostility had been directed at him.

He wasn't his father.

But Hank Walker had made one thing crystal clear—in his opinion, Cort would always be a loser, no matter how many wins he had under his belt.

Pushing the unpleasant thought aside, Cort gathered up

his rope and limped toward the chutes. He couldn't help but look toward the stands where he had reserved seating for guests. Emmaline Claiborne hadn't come the previous night, not that he'd really expected her to. Anyone with eyes could see that cowboys and rodeos definitely weren't her thing. He'd have done better to hawk the tickets on the street and pocket the money, like some of the other bull riders had done. Giving her those tickets had been a shot in the dark, and he told himself he had no reason to feel let down. But as his eyes scanned the section where the seats were located, he found himself coming to a stop.

She had turned up, after all.

Surprised didn't begin to describe how he felt. Hope flared briefly inside him, and then dimmed just as swiftly. Just because she'd turned up that didn't mean she would want to see him outside of the rodeo event. The truth was he'd likely never see her again after tonight.

He mentally kicked himself—again—for not staying longer at the bar with her; for not schmoozing her the way his gut had told him to do. From the instant he saw her picture on the dating app, something had grabbed hold of him and refused to let go. He'd told her the truth about Rhys; they *were* childhood friends and a personal emergency *had* prevented Rhys from keeping his appointment with Emma—Cort refused to call it a date. But it had been Cort's idea to go meet Emmaline at the posh Manhattan bar and tell her that Rhys wouldn't be able to make it. He'd never before felt such a compulsion to meet someone; he knew the instant he saw her profile picture that there was something special about her. His only regret was that he'd never have the chance to get to know her the way he wanted to. Women like Emmaline Claiborne didn't fall for guys like him.

Now, catching his eye, she smiled and waved. He couldn't deny she was easy on the eyes, and her smile was infectious. On impulse, Cort tossed his hat, Frisbee-style, into the stands, toward her. She caught it, smiled even wider, and placed it on her head. The crowd cheered their approval. With a last wave, Cort jogged out of the arena, trying to pretend his leg wasn't causing him all kinds of hellish pain. He made his way through the staging area behind the bucking chutes, accepting the congratulatory handshakes and backslapping from the other bull riders and support staff. A sports reporter and cameraman from a national sports channel intercepted him.

"Cort Channing, how do you feel right now, knowing those eight seconds just put you on a very short list of bull riders?" the reporter asked.

"I feel pretty good," he replied, grinning. "It's been a special night."

"What were you thinking when you drew Hammer and Anvil, knowing the last thirty bull riders who tried to ride him had been bucked off in the first few seconds of their go-round?"

Cort pushed a hand through his hair and laughed. "I wasn't at all sure it would go the way it did, I can tell you that. He's a quick, athletic animal and I just did what I could to stay on."

"That ride just bumped you into the top twenty competitors, up from number thirty-four. That has got to be a good feeling."

"Absolutely." Cort nodded. "I have nothing but respect for the other competitors and for the bulls. I feel privileged to be here."

The reporter stepped closer. "Care to tell us about the pretty fan you tossed your hat to?"

Cort shrugged. "I only met her a couple of days ago, so I don't know her all that well, but I hope she keeps the hat. It looks a sight better on her."

"Thanks for taking time to talk to us. Good luck tomorrow night."

Free at last, Cort made his way through a maze of corridors behind the arena to the changing rooms. Dust, thick enough to leave footprints, covered the floors. Open lockers lined one wall, and a section of steel fencing had been mounted down the center of the room. Gear hung on the fencing, and several bull riders had wrapped their bull ropes around the top railing, and were working resin into their ropes, trying to make them as sticky as possible in order to improve their grip. Several cowboys lounged on nearby benches, watching the bull riding event on their phones. One rider dozed on a folding chair, while two others stretched, and a third did lunges down the hallway. Cort accepted several congratulations as he walked toward his locker, trying not to look as triumphant as he felt. He reminded himself that not every bull rider would have a successful ride that night and for some of them, this might be the end of the road. As if to mock his success, his hip and thigh began to throb where the bull had kicked him.

Standing in front of his locker, he untaped his riding glove and yanked it off, before unfastening the protective Kevlar vest that all cowboys wore during a ride. He dropped the gear onto the floor before unbuckling his leather chaps and laying them on the ground by his feet. His shirt was smeared with dirt and dung from his landing, so he peeled that off as well, and dropped it on top of the vest. Easing himself onto a nearby bench, he loosened the leather straps that he'd cinched around his boots, and then toed the boots off, wincing as his injured thigh protested. He'd have a spectacular bruise by morning, but at least it wouldn't put him out of commission for future events.

"Need to see the doc?"

Cort looked up to see a rodeo hand standing nearby, two ice packs and an Ace bandage in one hand, a bottle of aspirin in the other. Ty Jenkins was a former semi-professional bull rider who'd retired several years earlier due to an injury. These days, he frequented the various rodeo events, helping out behind the scenes. Ty knew every bull rider by name and was a source of encouragement and wisdom for many of the younger guys on the circuit.

"Nah, it'll be okay," Cort said, accepting the aspirin and swallowing them dry. At any arena, ice packs and bandages were as common as chaps and spurs, and he took them with a grunt of thanks. "I'll just keep ice on it for a while."

"Okay. That was a helluva ride."

Cort nodded. "Thanks."

As Ty ambled away, Cort stood and unbuckled his belt.

He pushed his jeans down over his hips and kicked them free until he stood in just his boxer briefs and socks. Twisting, he got a look at the back of his thigh. There, just beneath his right buttock, was a perfect imprint of the bull's hoof. The skin had turned a deep, angry red and had begun to swell.

Shit.

Scooping up the ice pack, he began limping toward the sports medicine room when he heard his name called. He turned to see Lane Barlow standing just inside the changing room. Beside him, wide-eyed and mouth partly open, stood Emmaline Claiborne, clutching his cowboy hat in her hands.

Shit. He'd wanted to see her again, but he hadn't envisioned this.

"Hey, Emmaline," he said, as if he was accustomed to greeting women wearing nothing but his briefs. "Enjoying the show?"

"What?" Her bug-eyed gaze, which had been traveling over his nearly naked body, snapped back up to his. Color swept into her neck and cheeks.

Cort hadn't meant the words the way she interpreted them, but found himself enjoying her sudden embarrassment. She wore an oversized red top that hit her midthigh, paired with artfully torn skinny jeans and high-heeled black boots. Through the rip in the material, he could see the pale skin of her thigh, reminding him how good she'd looked wearing that little black dress the other night. She'd probably never been to a rodeo event in her life, but Cort appreciated that she didn't look like every other woman at the arena, wearing a snap-front plaid shirt with jeans and Western boots.

"Oh my God. I'm sorry! I didn't mean to stare!" She raised a hand to her eyes, blocking her view of him. "I shouldn't be back here. I'll—I'll just leave."

It wasn't uncommon for wives or girlfriends to find their way to the dressing rooms following an event, but Cort had never had anyone, never mind someone as pretty as her, come looking for him. He didn't want Emmaline to leave.

"Nah, it's okay," he assured her. "Thanks for showing her back here, Lane."

"Figured if you gave her your hat, you wouldn't mind." The other man grinned, then left.

Emmaline blushed again and thrust the hat toward Cort. "Here. I know you didn't mean for me to keep it."

Tossing his hat to her had been impulsive, but it had seemed appropriate given that he'd just managed what had seemed an impossible feat eight seconds earlier. He had a couple of other hats, but none he liked as well as the gray Stetson she held in her hands. But instead of accepting it, he shook his head.

"No, you can have it. It looks better on you, anyway."

She smiled a slow, genuine smile and placed the hat on her head. "Thank you. And congratulations, by the way. You had a great ride."

"Thanks." Leaning down, he scooped his shirt from the bench, but not before he heard her gasp.

"Your leg! That looks painful." Her brows pulled together. "You should have someone look at that."

"It's fine." Tossing the soiled shirt into his locker, he

fished a clean one out of his duffel bag, aware of the amused glances they were drawing from the other cowboys in the room. "C'mon, you can help me."

"Me?" Her voice was almost a squeak. "I don't know anything about sports injuries."

But she followed him into the adjoining room where several padded metal tables had been set up for medical exams and massages. At the moment, there were no other cowboys in the room. Cort spread his shirt on the padded surface of the nearest table and then handed the Ace bandages to Emmaline.

"I'm going to hold the ice packs in place. Would you do me a favor and wrap that bandage around my leg to hold them there? I'd do it myself, but the angle is a little tricky."

She arched one eyebrow at him, but a smile lingered in the corners of her mouth. "You expect me to believe that? A guy who can hang on to a bucking bull can't manage a simple ice pack?"

Cort grinned, and held the ice against the back of his thigh. "C'mon, honey. Help a guy out?"

She chewed her lip, and then went down on one knee and began wrapping the stretchy bandage around his upper thigh. The brim of the cowboy hat concealed her face as she worked, but if he could see her, he'd bet she'd be blushing like crazy.

He widened his stance to give her room to work, but when it became clear she couldn't wrap the bandage around his thigh without coming into contact with his crotch, he took pity on her. Besides, if she kept it up and did actually brush her fingers against his balls, he wasn't sure he'd be able to hide his physical reaction. As it was, he was already getting hard.

"That's fine," he murmured, and brushed her hands aside. "I can take it from here."

She did look up at him then, and there was no mistaking the expression in her eyes.

She was as turned on as he was.

The knowledge did something to Cort. Heat gathered and pooled in his groin. She stood, rubbing her palms along the seat of her jeans, the movement causing the soft material of her top to pull taut across her full breasts. Cort turned his gaze away and focused instead on securing the ice pack. When he finished, he lowered himself onto his stomach on the bench, so that the ice pack sat on the back of his thigh.

"How long will you keep that on?" she asked.

Cort folded his arms beneath his chin. "About twenty minutes, then I need to get dressed and head back out to the arena to sign autographs. Why don't you pull up a chair and keep me company until then?"

He watched as she dragged a folding chair over and sat down near the end of the bench, where he could see her. She seemed uncertain.

"What's on your mind?"

"I had no idea you were a bull rider. Why didn't you tell me that the other night?"

Cort lifted his shoulders in a shrug. "It didn't seem important. I figured if you were interested in seeing me again, you'd show up."

A half smile tilted her mouth. "Pretty sure of yourself, aren't you, cowboy?"

"You're here, aren't you?"

She held his gaze for a long moment, and then looked down at her hands. "I guess I am."

Cort watched her, sensing her indecision. Was she thinking about Rhys? Did she feel guilty for coming out to see him, when just two days earlier she'd been all dolled up for his buddy? Cort didn't know the first thing about Emmaline, aside from what she'd put on her dating app profile, but he was sure of one thing: Rhys wasn't the right man for her. Even if Maisey Wade hadn't shown up on Rhys's doorstep two nights earlier, claiming to be pregnant with his baby, Rhys would have never made a woman like Emmaline Claiborne happy. They were as different as salt and sugar. Cort probably wasn't the right man for her, either, but he was selfish enough to want to try.

"So why'd you come out tonight, Emmaline?"

She raised her head, and her gaze was so dark and intense that Cort felt a shiver of something—apprehension or maybe anticipation—run through him. The feeling was a little like waiting in the chute area to mount a bull, not knowing what might happen, only that it was going to be a helluva ride.

"I have a favor to ask you. A *huge* favor." She continued to look at him, her expression both hopeful and wary.

"I'm listening." Aware that his muscles had tightened, Cort forced himself to relax.

"I don't know how to say this, so I'm just going to come right out with it." She drew in a deep breath. "Would you be my date to my sister's wedding in three weeks' time, in Texas?"

His surprise must have been evident because she leaned forward, putting her hands up to forestall whatever words he might say, although he couldn't have formed a response at that moment if his life depended on it. He'd been racking his brain, trying to think of some way to see her again if she didn't show up at the rodeo. Rhys had told him that her family owned a cattle ranch in Texas, less than thirty miles from where Cort and Rhys had grown up in Bandera. He'd been hopeful that they might have more in common than her fancy Manhattan image indicated.

"Don't say no yet," she begged. "Just let me tell you the details, and then you can think about it. But not for too long, because I need an answer by tomorrow."

"Tomorrow? You ask me to go to a wedding halfway across the country, and you want my answer *tomorrow*?" He gave a huff of disbelief, seeing his opportunity to sweet-talk Emmaline into his bed dry up like a cow flap under the Texas sun. "Sorry, sweetheart, but no can do. In case it's escaped you, I'm chasing a championship. I have an event in Oregon in two weeks."

"And the week after that?" she persisted. "Do you have something scheduled then?"

He didn't, not yet. But that didn't mean he couldn't still throw his name into the hat for one of the many bull riding events around the country. But his own plans aside, he was curious, both about Emmaline and her proposal. Propping his chin on his fist, he studied her. There had to be an ex involved. Some shit-for-brains who was too stupid to know what he'd let get away. "Why would you want to bring a complete stranger to your sister's wedding?"

She caught her lower lip in her teeth and for just a second, he thought her chin trembled. But then she drew in a breath and gave him a brilliant smile. "My little sister is marrying my ex."

For a moment, Cort could only stare at her, unable to comprehend what she'd just said. Emmaline put on a brave front, but Cort was neither heartless nor blind. He could see how hard it was for her to even say the words out loud.

"Had you two already broken things off when they began dating?" he asked, but looking at her face, he already knew the answer. He watched as Emmaline ducked her head and laced her fingers together. Finally, she shook her head.

Her ex had left her for her younger sister.

He hoped that sister never needed a kidney.

"Ouch."

She grimaced. "Exactly. I doubt I would have been invited to the wedding except that, well, we're *sisters.* She can't exclude me, and I can't refuse to go, at least not without looking like a sore loser." She leaned forward in her chair. "But there's no way I can go alone, not for an entire weekend. How sad and pathetic would I look if I showed up by myself? I can't do it." She shuddered. "It would be too humiliating."

"And because they're getting hitched, everyone has conveniently forgotten how they cheated."

She stared at him in astonishment. "Yes. Exactly. It's

been a year, but nobody seems to remember that they only got together at my expense." She paused. "Even as kids, she always wanted whatever I had. I didn't care when it was just my shoes or a pair of jeans, but she had to have Damon too. And now I have to smile and get them a nice wedding gift, and act like none of it bothers me. It totally sucks."

"So you need…what? A date? A fake boyfriend?"

"Something like that." She paused. "Rhys was my last hope for a date, but well…you know how that turned out."

"So now I'm your last hope?"

Cort didn't like being second-best. He liked to be the front-runner in whatever he did. The knowledge that he was even less than second-best—that he was a last resort—was more than a little off-putting. On the other hand, there was something irresistible about being a woman's last hope, and actually coming through for her. That appealed to the romantic in him. He thought about her request, about spending a weekend with her and her family, pretending they were a couple.

"Will you do it? You'd be saving my life, and my pride." She gave a self-deprecating laugh. "At least, what's left of it."

"You don't even know me. I could be exactly the kind of man your momma warned you about."

"I have good instincts," she said airily. "I know you're a decent person."

Cort barely contained a snort of laughter. The truth was, she knew nothing about him. If she did, she would never have approached him. He was tainted goods. No better than his grifter father, if his granddad was to be believed. But he was just selfish enough to want to do it.

"If I agree, what's in it for me?"

"What do you mean?" Her voice held equal notes of alarm and indignation. "I thought you were a gentleman."

Cort gave a small huff of laughter. "C'mon. You can't be that naïve."

"What is it you want?"

You.

The thought came out of nowhere, and for a moment, he was too startled by the revelation to reply. But even as she waited for him to respond, he realized it was the truth. Emmaline Claiborne was a beautiful, vibrant woman, and he'd be lying if he said he wasn't strongly attracted to her. But there was also a vulnerability to her that aroused a protective instinct in him. He wanted to keep her safe.

Hell, he just wanted to keep her.

But guys like him didn't get to keep women like Emmaline.

"Just so I'm clear," he continued, "are we romantically involved? Or will you introduce me as your platonic friend?"

Color seeped into her cheeks and she swallowed hard. "My preference is for us to look like a real couple. Like two people who are, you know, in love. Maybe."

"So you're expecting us to be physical with each other, at least in front of the happy couple." Cort felt himself warming to the idea.

"Affectionate."

"So we'd touch and kiss, and do all the things people do when they're in an *intimate* relationship. Just so I'm getting your meaning."

She made a small strangled sound, and then cleared her throat. "Well, yes. But only in front of other people. Obviously, you don't have to keep up the pretense when we're alone."

"And will we be? Alone?"

She looked suddenly flustered, which he shouldn't have found so charming. "We'll have separate rooms, if that's what you're asking. I can't imagine why we'd ever really be alone together."

Cort raised an eyebrow and allowed a small smile to curve his mouth. She was being deliberately naïve, but the air between them was suddenly thick and heavy. "Can't you?"

The vein throbbed along the side of her neck and she curled her hands against her thighs. He heard her swift indrawn breath and the way her gaze suddenly riveted on him.

"I'll pay for your expenses, of course. Whatever you need. It would only be for a long weekend." Her voice sounded weak. Breathless. "A three-day pretend relationship. After that, you're free."

Cort smiled. Accustomed to having just eight seconds, his imagination took off at a full stampede with the possibilities of what he could do in three days.

"Okay," he replied, trying to sound casual even as adrenaline pumped hard through his veins. "You've got yourself a boyfriend."

Chapter Three

A SUITCASE LAY open on Emma's bed, surrounded by a colorful heap of dresses, skirts, and flowing pants, some half slithering off the bed to the floor. Emma barely noticed the mess. She stood in the middle of her walk-in closet, sorting through the dozens of outfits in near despair.

What *did* one wear to a small-town Texas wedding when you were related to the bride and had once been in a relationship with the groom? When the entire town remembered how the bride's mother had wrecked your parents' marriage, much like how the bride herself had managed to destroy your own hopes and dreams? When every guest there would be watching you? Judging you? Maybe even secretly hoping for a cat fight between the Claiborne sisters?

The enormity of what lay ahead suddenly seemed too much to bear. Emma had been holding a deep blue cocktail dress in one hand, and now she returned it to the clothes rack with a sinking sense of despair. She couldn't do it. She couldn't subject herself to the snide whisperings and sympathetic glances, and she especially couldn't endure her sister's gloating expression of triumph. Her family expected too much of her. Emma's throat tightened, and the hot sting of tears pricked her eyes.

She couldn't go. She *wouldn't* go. Even the enticement of showing up with a super-hot cowboy wasn't incentive enough for what she would have to suffer. She'd rather go to the dentist and have her gums scraped until they bled than endure the humiliation of the upcoming wedding.

Her dismal musings were interrupted by the strident buzz of her doorbell. With a sense of relief, Emma hastily wiped her damp eyes with the hem of her shirt sleeve, and left the war zone that was her bedroom. On the closed-circuit display beside her entry door, she could see her mother standing in the lobby of the building, staring directly into the camera with a look of impatience on her face.

Emma groaned. She definitely was not in the mood to deal with her mother. Natalie Germaine had already expressed her opinion about Emma attending the wedding, and now she had stopped by to drive her point home yet again. Mentally bracing herself, Emma pressed the button that would allow her mother to ride the elevator to the top floor of the renovated industrial building Emma rented.

"Darling, you look awful," Natalie said in greeting as she pressed a perfunctory kiss on Emma's cheek before breezing past her into the apartment, leaving a soft cloud of Clive Christian No. 1 perfume in her wake.

"Thanks, Mom." Raising her eyebrows and drawing in a deep breath, Emma closed the door and followed her mother into the kitchen, watching as Natalie plunked her expensive handbag onto the center island and glanced around with a critical eye. She looked every inch the elegant, affluent New

Yorker. Her dark hair was cut in a sleek, stacked bob, and her makeup was flawless. Removing her coat, Natalie dropped it over the back of a bar stool. She wore a pair of lightweight, cream woolen slacks paired with a sleeveless black turtleneck that showed her toned arms to advantage. Emma glanced down at her own baggy sweatpants and oversized football jersey, feeling like a grungy teenager.

"Have you done something different in here?" The question sounded almost accusatory.

Reaching for two wineglasses, Emma tried to imagine the spacious brick-and-beam loft apartment through her mother's eyes. "I don't think so. I hung some of my paintings since the last time you were here, so maybe that's what looks different."

"Hmm." Natalie strolled across the kitchen to study a large canvas of abstract flower blooms. "This is rather nice."

Emma gave a wry smile as she opened a bottle of white wine and poured them each a glass. "Thanks, Mom." She handed her mother a glass and they stood in contemplative silence for a moment, looking at the painting.

"Well," Natalie finally said, turning to Emma. "How are you feeling about this weekend?"

The wedding.

Emma took a hefty swig of her wine and nodded confidently. "Good. I'm feeling good."

"Hmm." That simple vocalization spoke volumes. "You don't have to go, you know that, right?"

"Mom." Emma gave her mother a tolerant look. "I can't *not* go. Whatever you may think of her, Callie is still my sister."

"*Half* sister." Ignoring Emma's warning look, she shrugged. "I just think, under the circumstances, you could make your excuses and not put yourself through what's going to be a very stressful experience. A nightmare, really. No one would blame you for bowing out. She may be your half sister, but she's not family. Not really. Sisters don't steal each other's boyfriends. She sent you an invitation out of duty, but I'm sure she's hoping you won't show up." She paused. "Or maybe she is, just to see you suffer."

"I'm going to the wedding, Mom, if only to hold my head up and show them they haven't gotten the best of me. I'd think you, of all people, would understand that."

Natalie's eyes narrowed. "Your father and I were already having trouble when that...that *woman* took advantage of the situation. We might have gotten through the rough patch in our marriage if she hadn't gotten her hooks into him, and then gotten pregnant." One manicured fingernail tapped against the goblet of her wineglass. "And now history is repeating itself. The apple didn't fall far from the Rachel Dean tree, did it?"

Emma had heard all of this before. Repeatedly.

"First of all, Damon and I weren't having problems before Callie spent the summer with us," Emma protested. "Everything was *fine*. I blame myself for not taking time off from work to spend with her. I left her alone too much, and put the burden on Damon to keep her entertained."

"Oh, *please*." Her mother swung away and began walking toward Emma's bedroom. "I don't know why you're so willing to make excuses for their appalling behavior. But since you're so determined to make a martyr of yourself and see this through, the least I can do is ensure you're dressed appropriately."

"Mom, wait—" Emma watched as her mother stopped in the doorway of the bedroom and surveyed the scene.

"Seems I was just in time," Natalie said, and strolled over to the bed, holding her wineglass in one hand as she picked through the assortment of discarded clothing on the bed, assessing each piece before tossing it aside. "No, no, and most definitely no."

"Mom, I can dress myself."

Natalie reached into the suitcase and withdrew a pair of designer denim jeans and held them up. "Really? You can't do better than this?"

"It's a ranch, Mom. Except for the wedding ceremony, that's what everyone else will be wearing."

"That's fine for everyone else, but not for you." She dropped the denim pants onto the floor and set her wineglass down on the bedside table. "You want to show them that they didn't get the best of you? You'll need to do better than blue jeans. Because you're not fine; you're *spectacular*."

Emma watched as her mother walked over to the spacious closet and began rifling through the clothes hangers, considering each garment with careful deliberation. "This," she said, pulling a slinky black jumpsuit from the rack and tossing it to Emma. "And this. And definitely this little number."

"*Mom.*"

"What?" Natalie looked at her daughter, her expression one of innocent surprise.

"None of these outfits are appropriate!"

Natalie's mouth flattened. "You aren't going to the wedding so you can be appropriate. You're going to be *unforgettable.* Do you really want to send a message? Make a statement?" When Emma didn't immediately respond, Natalie pressed on. "It's time you showed them who you are, Emma, and you're not a Texan. You never will be. You're barely even a Claiborne. You have Germaine blood running through your veins, and that means you're a New Yorker, through and through. The only boots you wear are Gucci."

While her mother meant well, her words caused an unfamiliar tightening in Emma's chest. She thought of her three older half brothers and her father. Last Stand, Texas, was in their blood; the Claiborne family had lived there since the actual last stand had taken place in 1836, giving the town its iconic name. The Claibornes had been ranchers then, and they were ranchers now. Getting covered in mud, dust, and cow manure was an expected side effect of running a cattle ranch. While the Claiborne family had managed to accumulate a modest amount of wealth, the men were down to earth and unpretentious. They wouldn't understand if Emma showed up wearing a pair of black jeggings and high-heeled boots. They'd think she was a pompous snob.

Emma loved her mother; they'd supported each other for as long as she could remember. While part of her understood her mother's opposition to anything Texan, another part of her longed for the family she'd left behind. She didn't want to stand apart. She wanted, more than anything, to belong to that family. Not that anyone had ever asked her what she wanted. She'd been little more than a toddler when her parents had separated, and her father had allowed Natalie to take Emma away to New York. But for as long as Emma could remember, her mother had worried that Gus Claiborne would use his money to sue Natalie for full custody of their daughter.

Only he never had.

After Emma turned eighteen and graduated from high school, Natalie had fretted about the possibility of Gus trying to entice Emma back to Last Stand with promises of a generous allowance, or a lucrative job, or any number of other bribes.

But he hadn't done that, either.

Emma drew in a deep breath. She'd always found it hard to oppose her mother, especially when it came to her father and siblings. Her mother worried about her every time she went to Texas, but she wasn't a child anymore. She was a grown woman, capable of making her own decisions. "I just don't want to be a laughingstock if I show up wearing designer clothing when everyone else is wearing denim and plaid shirts."

Natalie continued sorting through Emma's clothing. "One can never be overdressed, darling, and nobody has ever laughed at Saint Laurent or Prada, trust me on that."

"But maybe I'd be more comfortable in something less *showy*."

"Nothing is as comfortable as good quality clothing."

Releasing the garment she'd been holding, she turned to confront Emma. "Why is it so important for you to dress according to their standards? What have any of them ever done for you?"

"Mom, please," Emma murmured. She knew that tone, and it didn't bode anything good. Natalie frequently grew indignant on her behalf, thinking Emma was being shortchanged by her father, but conversely, she did everything in her power to ensure Emma remained in New York, or at least didn't fit easily into the Claiborne clan. Emma was tired of the endless back and forth. "I'll wear whatever you think is best."

But Natalie wasn't going to be deterred. "No, really, I want to know. Your wardrobe is good enough for New York, good enough for your friends, good enough for your job at the gallery, but suddenly it's not good enough for the almighty Claiborne family? Or maybe it's too good, and you want to dumb yourself down for them?"

"No, that's not it at all," Emma protested. "I just think I'll look like a fish out of water if I wear this stuff."

Stepping closer, Natalie cupped Emma's face in her hands. "You don't have to conform to their standards, darling. You're my daughter, and nothing they do will ever change that."

"I know that, Mom, and I don't want to change that." Emma had heard it all before. But her mother had warmed to the subject, and now she picked up her glass of wine and took a healthy swallow before turning to Emma. "Do you have any idea how furious I am that they would even invite you to this wedding? Do you? When I think of *that woman* sitting in the front pew of the church, *rejoicing* because her daughter managed to break my daughter's heart, I just want to scream!"

Natalie had always been friendly to Callie, right up until the point when she'd run off with Emma's boyfriend. But that had changed the second she'd seen Emma's tears. While Emma understood her mother's indignation came from a place of love, she wasn't in the mood for it. "I know, Mom. It's okay," she soothed. "I'll be fine, I promise."

"It wasn't enough that your father had to humiliate me, but now he wants to humiliate you, as well! It's too much! He demands too much! He's never even been a real father to you, and now he expects you to just suck it up, like it's *completely normal* for your half sister to marry your former boyfriend!" She made a slashing motion with her free hand. "It's sick, I tell you. *Twisted*."

"It's okay, Mom." Emma put her arms around her mother, feeling the familiar need to comfort and protect her. "Like you said before, Callie and I aren't close. It's not like we even saw each other all that much growing up. It's obvious to me now that Damon and I weren't suited to each other, and I was the only one who couldn't see it. If it hadn't been Callie, it would have been someone else."

Even if she didn't believe her own words, they seemed to mollify Natalie. With a deep sigh, her mother pulled out of Emma's embrace and smiled apologetically.

"I only want what's best for you, you know that, right?"

"Of course I do."

Reaching out, Natalie brushed back a loose tendril of Emma's dark hair, her expression one of wry humor. "You're a Germaine, darling. Remember that. You belong to one of the finest families in the Hudson Valley. So what if some Claiborne ancestor holed up in a saloon and helped fight off the Mexican army? Who has ever heard of Daughters of the Last Stand, anyway? You're a Daughter of the American Revolution! A descendant of a true patriot!"

Emma smiled, as she knew her mother had meant for her to. Natalie didn't really care about any of those lofty organizations, but it had become something of a private joke between them, especially since Natalie had refused her own mother's urgings to become a member of the Daughters of the Revolution.

Now Natalie sighed. "I just wish you didn't have to go alone. I'd go with you if I thought I wouldn't be tossed out on my rear, but even if I had been invited, I don't think I can leave the gallery unattended."

"I'm not going alone. I have a date, so you don't have to worry."

Dropping her hands, Natalie stepped back, surprise evident in her dark eyes. "Really? Why am I only hearing about this now?"

"He—my date—only agreed to go with me recently."

"Anybody I know?"

Emma recalled again that moment when Cort had walked into the restaurant and all eyes had turned to him, including hers. His good looks had been striking, his confidence impressive. But none of that mattered. Her mother would have a conniption if she realized Emma was bringing a bull rider to the wedding, especially since she'd spent most of Emma's life warning her against cowboys and their many vices. A bull rider would be that much worse, since her mother would no doubt view Cort as even more inferior and unruly than a simple cowboy. Unbidden, an image of Cort in all his half-naked glory returned to her. His lean body had been layered in muscle, his skin warmed to a silken tan by the sun, and her fingers had itched to explore the hard ridges of his cobbled stomach.

Her mother had been right; cowboys were dangerous.

"No," she replied in response to her mother's query. "He's…a friend of a friend, but he seems nice and he understands the situation."

"That's good; I'm glad you have someone to go with. I hope he comes from a good family, although the Claibornes wouldn't recognize real class if it jumped up and bit them on their rears. Just be sure you understand the situation too."

Emma didn't point out that she was a Claiborne. "What does that mean?"

"You don't belong there, sweetie. You need to keep that in mind while you're there. Your father may try to persuade you to stay, but you belong here." Natalie paused, and for a moment Emma saw something like sadness and maybe even regret in her eyes. "You'll be tempted to stay. There's a beauty to the place; an allure that's hard to describe."

Emma thought of Riverrun, the family ranch that lay sprawled along the banks of the Pedernales River, shaded by live oaks and cypress trees. As a child, she'd always loved the ranch. The weeks leading up to her school vacations had been filled with anticipation of returning to Last Stand, of seeing her father and siblings and their housekeeper, Rosa-Maria, and of riding the horse that her father had given her on her tenth birthday. Nothing had been as wonderful as cantering through the Hill Country with her brothers and father. Of course, she couldn't tell her mother any of that.

"I know. I've been there before," Emma reminded her gently. "Many times."

"You were young then. You haven't been back to Last Stand in years. Now that you're grown, you'll see everything through different eyes. You'll fall in love with the ranch and the lifestyle, but it's an illusion. The reality is far different and not nearly as pretty."

Emma had actually visited Last Stand just two years earlier, with Damon, but she wasn't going to bring that up. Natalie rarely talked about the days when she'd fallen for a cowboy and left her affluent life in the city to become a rancher's wife. Emma wasn't surprised the marriage hadn't lasted; her mother wasn't cut out for life on a working cattle ranch. She'd been indulged and pampered her entire life. She craved attention and constant affirmations of love, and that wasn't Gus Claiborne's style.

"I'll be fine, Mom. Trust me when I say I'm in no danger of falling in love with anything or anyone in Texas."

But as she helped her mother select the outfits she would bring with her to the wedding, she had a sudden image of Cort Channing's sea-green eyes and lovely mouth, and the way he had looked at her when he'd agreed to be her pretend boyfriend.

Thank goodness cowboys were off her list. His easy confidence and sexy smile would doubtless have the female guests swooning with desire, but she would be in absolutely no danger of succumbing to his manly charms.

Chapter Four

E MMA SENT UP a small prayer of thanks when she spotted
Cort making his way purposefully toward the baggage
carousel at the San Antonio airport two days later. Her own
flight from New York had arrived an hour earlier, and she
and Cort had arranged to meet at the baggage claim area and
drive together to Last Stand. Until that moment, Emma
hadn't been sure he would actually make good on his
promise to go with her to the wedding. They'd talked on the
phone several times—he'd actually called her—and while
their conversations had been brief, he'd left her laughing
every time. If possible, his voice had sounded even more
smoky-rough on the phone than it did in person, and she
hated to admit how much she had been looking forward to
seeing him again.

And now here he was, looking even more like a rugged
cowboy than she remembered. He wore a snap-front shirt in
a bold plaid, and a pair of Wranglers that hugged his hips,
and Emma didn't miss how more than one woman turned
for a second look as he walked past. Cort Channing wasn't
an overly tall man, but he was solidly and perfectly propor-
tioned, with broad shoulders that tapered to lean hips and

powerful thighs. Just the recollection of the muscles that lay hidden beneath those Wranglers caused Emma's mouth to go a little dry. To her everlasting shame and secret pleasure, she'd thought of little else but Cort—in his boxer briefs—during the past three weeks.

As if some sixth sense alerted him, Cort turned and their eyes met. A smile curved his mouth, and he lifted one hand to touch the brim of his hat. Forcing herself to ignore the nervous fluttering in her stomach, Emma made her way through the throngs of travelers toward him, pulling her oversized suitcase behind her, and hitching her Gucci tote bag higher onto her shoulder. She was glad now that she'd taken care with her appearance. She'd chosen a pair of narrow, black ankle pants paired with a loose blouse that slid artfully off one shoulder, revealing a lace-edged, feminine tank top beneath. But maybe the ankle booties with the stiletto heels had been a mistake, because her feet were already killing her. Cort watched her approach, his expression inscrutable. Emma's nerves were stretched taut by the time she reached his side.

"How was your flight?" Had she really thought he wasn't a physically imposing man? He was only about six inches taller than herself, with his boots adding another inch or two, but the breadth of his shoulders and the expression in his eyes made her feel unaccountably small, and very aware of her own femininity.

"No complaints."

The mildness of his tone was in such direct contrast to the intensity of his gaze that tiny explosions of awareness went off inside her, as bright and effervescent as sparklers on a summer night. She felt momentarily dazzled.

"Good." She gestured vaguely toward his duffel bag and the single garment bag he had slung over his shoulder, and strove to sound casual and unaffected. "Is that all you brought? Did you check any luggage?"

"No, ma'am. When you travel as much as I do, you learn to pack light." He looked meaningfully at her enormous suitcase, and Emma thought she saw a hint of amusement in his eyes.

"A girl needs options," she said lamely. At her mother's urging, she had literally brought everything in her arsenal, including the sexy red number she had bought on a whim in the hope of reigniting some passion in her flagging relationship with Damon. But on the night she had planned to wear the dress, Damon had announced he was leaving her.

For her younger sister.

Emma had never worn the dress. Instead, she'd stayed home alone, burying her misery and confusion deep in a container of rocky road ice cream.

"Uh-huh." Those two drawled syllables told Emma he wasn't fooled. Cort knew exactly why she'd brought such a big suitcase.

"So how did you do at your bull riding event last weekend?" she asked, striving to switch the topic to something safer. More benign. Because this man had a way of seeing too much, and she had a crazy, uncharacteristic urge to tell him more than he needed to know, both about herself, her relief at seeing him, and her gnawing anxiety about the coming weekend.

"Not bad," he said. "I had two good rides with high scores, so I'm hopeful I'll make it to the invitationals in Las Vegas at the end of the year." He gave her a wink. "I just need to stay healthy and injury-free."

His words brought back the ever-present memory of him standing in his boxer briefs, with a brilliant bruise blooming on the back of his thigh.

His rock-hard, muscular thigh.

Emma cleared her throat. "So, um, your leg is doing better?"

Cort paused in the act of reaching down to retrieve his duffel bag, and pinioned her with a knowing look. "Yes, ma'am. You let me know if you'd like to check it out for yourself."

With a grin, he slung the duffel bag over his shoulder. Before Emma could guess his intent, he took the handle of her suitcase from her unresisting fingers and began walking toward the exit doors, leaving her with no option but to follow him. She might have protested, but the sight of his very fine butt in those Wranglers had apparently stolen her ability to speak. Or think. Or do anything except trail behind him in mute admiration.

Thirty minutes later, Cort had their luggage stowed in the back of a shiny new Ford F150 and was expertly navigating the big vehicle toward Interstate 10. As the urban sprawl of San Antonio fell away behind them, she resisted the urge to put the window down and stick her head outside just to feel the wind against her face, the way she'd done as a little girl. The countryside grew more rural, and she relished the sight of the rolling hills. Overhead, the sky was a deep, cloudless blue and the fields beside the highway were an endless sweep of swaying grasses, punctuated by stands of live oaks. Emma had forgotten how vast the Texas countryside was.

Every drive from the airport to the ranch seemed like the beginning of a great adventure. Her father had always come to collect her, and he could never drive to Last Stand quick enough for her. Now, however, the thought of what—*of who*—awaited her at Riverrun Ranch made her stomach clench with dread.

She gave a start when Cort reached over and covered her hand with his, curling his warm fingers around hers and giving them a reassuring squeeze. "Relax. Everything is going to be fine."

"Do I look nervous?"

Her voice came out as a squeak, not surprising since every nerve ending in her body was squealing because he was *touching* her.

He gave a soft chuckle, but he didn't release her hand. "Actually, you do, yeah."

She *was* nervous, only now it had nothing to do with returning to Last Stand, or attending the wedding, and everything to do with the sensations that were racing from that bright point where their hands were joined, through her entire body. She couldn't remember ever having such an immediate and visceral reaction to a man's touch. Even Damon had never made her feel so jumpy or self-conscious.

She reminded herself that she didn't know Cort, and she certainly was *not* attracted to him. Hadn't she promised herself she would never fall for a cowboy? Besides which, she wasn't looking. Definitely *not* looking.

He withdrew his hand, and Emma was able to breathe again. But she couldn't stop herself from covertly studying him as he drove. His profile was clean and strong beneath the brim of his hat, and in the close confines of the truck cab, he seemed even larger. And with barely a foot of space between them, she realized she could *smell* him. The combination of clean laundry detergent, spicy soap, and warm undertones of leather was a heady mixture. Emma was tempted to lean in closer and breathe deeply. Instead, she sat primly upright with her hands resting lightly on her lap.

"I still don't understand why we couldn't just drive the car I'd reserved," she said in an effort to change the subject. Cort had insisted upon exchanging the sedan she'd requested for the rugged, albeit beautifully appointed, pickup truck.

"I may only be your fake boyfriend," he said, slanting her a rueful smile, "and maybe I'll never see any of these people again, but I still have my pride. This is Texas, and there's no way I'm showing up on your family's ranch in some sissy hybrid. Your brothers would run me off the property with a shotgun."

Emma glanced curiously at him. "Did you know my great-great-grandfather a couple of times over was called Sherman 'Shotgun' Claiborne?"

Cort laughed. "No. How'd he get that name?"

"Rumor has it he kidnapped the beautiful daughter of a

local Mexican family and forced her at gunpoint to marry him. Nobody has ever been able to prove if the story is true, but our family history shows more than one wedding took place at the business end of a shotgun."

A burst of surprised laughter escaped Cort, and he glanced at Emma. "Should I be worried?"

"Thankfully, the Claiborne men have evolved a little bit over the last two centuries. But how do you know I have brothers? I don't recall mentioning any siblings, other than my sister."

"Darlin', I never enter an arena without at least some inkling of what to expect. You can find out pretty much anything about anyone on the internet." He cast her a quick grin. "But feel free to tell me whatever you think I need to know about your family."

The knowledge that he'd performed an internet search on the Claiborne family surprised Emma. She hadn't thought this weekend meant anything more to him than a few free meals and a chance to spin her around a dance floor. Emma turned sideways in her seat to face him, resting her back against the passenger door. She tilted her head and eyed him with interest. "Now I'm curious. What, exactly, did you learn?"

He cast her a quick glance before looking back at the road. "You already told me your family has been in Last Stand for generations, since the original standoff with some Mexican troops back in the 1830s."

"Right. My great-great-great-granddaddy—Shotgun Claiborne, the one I was telling you about—was one of the original defenders of the Last Stand Saloon, where the fighting took place." She paused, then asked, "And what else did you learn?"

"I know your family owns a pretty piece of land along the river, with six hundred head of cattle. Your daddy has done well for himself."

"Well, I'm not sure about the number of cattle, but the ranch does overlook the river." The main house sat on a knoll overlooking the water. How many picnic lunches had her father's housekeeper, Rosa-Maria, packed for them to enjoy by the river's edge, beneath the shade of the cypress trees? As a child, Emma had spent hours climbing on the rocks and splashing in the shallows of the limestone canyon with her twin brothers, catching water-skimmers and tiny silver fish. Now she pushed the memories aside. "And..."

She watched as Cort shifted in his seat, and then cleared his throat. "I think it's fair to say your family doesn't have a great track record where marriage is concerned." He flashed her a quick grin. "Now I'm thinking it could be the whole shotgun thing. Your daddy was married three times, and your younger sister..." He trailed off, giving her an apologetic glance. "Your sister was conceived while he was still hitched to your mother."

Emma had to clamp her mouth shut to stem the spontaneous words of defense that sprang to her lips. Her whole life, she'd listened to her mother malign Gus Claiborne, and rail about the unfairness of how he'd thrown their marriage down the toilet for a cheap piece of ass. But she'd learned early on that nothing good came of trying to defend either

her father or his actions. He *had* been unfaithful. He *had* fathered a child outside of his marriage.

"Did you know the Claiborne family motto is *Do the right thing*?" she asked. Her mouth curved into a rueful smile. "Of course, my father would never let someone else define him, so he probably had an affair just to thumb his nose at his ancestors. Anyway, my parents have been divorced for over twenty years. I'm sure the whole affair was scandalous at the time, but it's old news. Did you find out anything else?"

"I know you have three brothers." He ticked them off on his fingers. "Holt is the oldest. He's also divorced, and he works as the ranch manager. His mother died when he was born, but your daddy remarried pretty quickly. Gus and his second wife had twin boys, Luke and Evan, but she bailed when the boys were still toddlers, found herself a semi-pro ball player and went on the road with him. Not the kind of life for little boys, so they stayed with their daddy on the ranch. Luke is in the army, and Evan works with Holt, managing the day-to-day operations on the ranch, when he's not volunteering for the local fire department." He slid her a sideways look. "How'm I doing so far?"

"Well, you've done your homework. I'm impressed."

"Actually, I didn't have to dig too deep," Cort admitted. "I came across an interview Holt did with *Cattleman Quarterly* last year. He was pretty candid about his childhood, and life on the ranch. But he didn't mention you." Cort looked over at her, and his gaze was thoughtful. "When's the last time you were in Texas?"

A pang of regret and something that felt like loss knifed through Emma. Holt hadn't mentioned her in the article because her connection to the Claiborne family was peripheral, at best. When her parents' marriage crumbled, her mother fled to New York and took three-year-old Emma with her. She hadn't been a part of the family—a real part—in a very long time.

"It's been a while," she admitted. "I used to come here every chance I got when I was a kid, every school and summer vacation. My father always made a big deal when I came to visit. There were horse rides and picnics and county fairs. I can't believe I'm admitting this, but I even liked being teased by my brothers. Everything in Last Stand was so different than my life in the city. But..." She shrugged. "Once I got to be a teenager, there was always something to prevent me from coming back. School activities, friends...boys."

My mother.

"So we're talking years?"

Emma shifted forward in her seat and looked out the window at the passing countryside, but didn't really see it. "I came back for Christmas two and a half years ago, when my mother decided to go to Hawaii for the holidays. Growing up, I'd alternate who I spent Christmas with every year. One year I'd stay in New York, and the next year I'd come to Last Stand. That was the agreement my parents made during their divorce settlement. I pretty much stopped coming to Texas when I turned eighteen and could make my own decisions, but I always came back for Christmas every other year."

She'd brought Damon to Last Stand with her that Christmas, and that had been the first time he'd met her father and brothers. The first time he'd met Callie. Emma had been so proud, introducing him to her family, and so naïve, thinking what they'd shared had been special. A once-in-a-lifetime kind of love.

She'd been such an idiot.

She should have known better. Hadn't her parents' experiences taught her anything? That kind of cosmic connection didn't exist. She had her doubts about whether or not Callie's marriage to Damon would last, given the foundation of lies and betrayal they'd built their relationship on. Come to think of it, Damon had been the one to suggest she invite Callie to New York that following summer, after they'd spent Christmas in Last Stand. He'd pushed the issue, even when Emma had protested that she couldn't take time off from work, and didn't want to leave Callie alone. Damon had swept her concerns aside, promising he would take good care of Callie and personally ensure she had a good time.

Boy, had he ever.

"Do your dad or your brothers ever come up to New York to see you?" Cort asked, interrupting her dark thoughts.

"They do, but less often now that I'm grown. My father would visit a few times every year, and sometimes he'd bring one or two of the boys with him. When I was in college, they'd fly up at least once a semester. I don't see Luke as often, since he doesn't have the luxury of taking time off whenever he wants. He's active duty, but once this last tour is over, he's getting out of the army for good. So I'm hoping I'll get to see more of him."

"That's good to hear," Cort said. "Family is important."

His words caused an ache in Emma's chest. She hadn't felt like part of the Claiborne family in a very long time, and since Callie and Damon had announced their engagement, she'd avoided coming back to Last Stand. She was an outsider, an itinerant member of the family, and everyone would probably breathe a sigh of relief when she finally returned to New York. There was a part of her, too, that wanted to rail out at her father and brothers for not having her back when her own sister had pulled the rug out from under her life. Clearly, they were siding with Callie, as if getting married made everything okay. Blowing out a hard breath, Emma pushed the unhappy thoughts aside.

Cort switched on the radio and tuned it to a country station. He'd rolled his sleeves back over his forearms, and Emma found herself mesmerized by the play of muscles beneath his tanned skin. He was silent for several moments, listening to the music as his thumb tapped an absent rhythm on the steering wheel. He looked relaxed and completely unfazed by the idea of meeting her family. Emma envied him. She wished she felt half as confident as he looked.

"What about your own family?" she asked. "Are you close to them?"

His thumb stopped its idle drumming on the steering wheel, and for a moment, Emma didn't think he intended to answer.

"It's just me," he finally said. "I never knew my father, and my mom died in a car wreck when I was pretty young. I don't have many memories of her."

"I'm sorry," she apologized, dismayed by his admission, and embarrassed by her own tactlessness. "I had no idea, or I wouldn't have asked."

Cort shrugged. "It's fine. It was a long time ago."

"Who raised you?"

"My grandfather." His hand tightened on the steering wheel. "He passed about a year ago. Actually, it will be a year next week."

"Again, I'm sorry," Emma murmured. "Were you close?"

"Nope."

Just that single word—no clarification, and no details. But Emma thought she heard a world of hurt and regret in Cort's voice.

"What about your grandmother?"

"She passed before I was born."

"Is there anything else I should know?" she probed gently. "I mean, my family might ask questions and it's best if I know how to respond…"

"My granddad owned a ranch not too far from Last Stand, over in Bandera. He raised bucking bulls, and he bred some of the best bulls in the industry. I was obsessed with bull riding. I began working the amateur circuits as soon as I got out of high school. Granddad didn't approve. Even when I began winning, he wouldn't come watch me. We had words when I was about twenty-two, and I left for good."

"It must have been hard when you lost him."

"I hadn't spoken to him in five years, so I didn't know how bad it was until I got a call that he'd had a fall. He'd broken his hip, and had to go into a nursing home. But he never really recovered. He went downhill fast and was gone in six months." Cort shrugged. "After he died, the bank moved in and took everything."

"What? Why?"

"About the time my mother died, he suffered a…financial loss that set him back pretty hard. After he passed, I learned he hadn't paid taxes on his property in more than ten years. He'd also taken out a reverse mortgage, so technically, the bank owned his ranch." His hand tightened on the steering wheel, and a muscle flexed in his lean jaw. "I had no idea. I thought he was financially solvent. Of course, he never would have said anything to me, and he never would have wanted me to know that he was struggling."

"You can't blame yourself," she said softly, feeling a surge of sympathy for him. "You weren't responsible for his mistakes."

Cort made a sound of self-loathing. "I should have been there. I should have been more involved, but we didn't part on good terms. I knew he'd sold off his best bulls, but I just chalked it up to an old man getting ready for retirement." He was quiet for a moment. "I didn't know he was losing the ranch, but maybe that was all part of his grand plan. Right or wrong, he didn't want me to have the ranch, and this was his way of making sure I never would."

Emma was silent, shocked by his admission. What kind

of grandfather would raise a child, and then deliberately deny him what should have been his inheritance? She wondered what had happened between Cort and his grandfather to create such a rift.

"So where do you live now?"

"I rent a couple of rooms over a brew pub in Idaho," he replied. "My buddy owns the pub, so he gives me a deal. It's not much, but I'm not there very often. I like it because it's affordable, my buddy keeps an eye on the place when I'm away, and it ensures we stay in touch."

Emma thought she could see him living there, like an old-fashioned cowboy renting a room over a saloon. But Idaho was a long way from Bandera, Texas.

"Why do you think your grandfather didn't want you to have the ranch?"

"Oh, no, honey," he said gently, and slid her a warning glance. "That's a story I don't tell unless I'm good and drunk."

"Can you get it back?"

"I have some money saved, but I need to win big in the arena if I'm going to get enough to pay off the back taxes and loans he took out. The property is going on the auction block at the end of the year, so I'm hoping to make an offer to the bank before that happens."

"Does bull riding pay well?"

"Only if you win," he said with a soft laugh.

A thought occurred to her. "Are you well known in bull riding circles? I mean, my brothers love that stuff. Will they recognize you?"

Cort shifted his gaze back to the road. One shoulder hitched upward, as if shrugging off a mild annoyance. "Maybe. I don't know. I've been riding bulls since I was twelve, but I only started getting noticed recently."

"So it's possible they could recognize you," she persisted.

"Yeah, it's possible," he conceded. "Why? Is that a problem?"

"I can't tell my family that we only met a few weeks ago. They'd see this for what it is—a sham. They need to think we've been together for a while, and that we're serious."

Cort nodded, as if giving the dilemma serious thought. "Okay. I had a quick trip through New York last fall. We can say we met at a bar in Manhattan—which we did—but we'll just change up the timeline and say it was eight months ago."

"That could work," Emma said. "Why were you in New York?"

He slanted her a swift, apologetic glance. "I was visiting Rhys. He was going through a rough patch, so we pretty much spent a long weekend getting drunk."

Emma barely restrained the urge to roll her eyes. "So we'll say we met that weekend, and we've had a long-distance romance ever since. I made a couple of trips to the west coast to visit art galleries over the winter. We can say we spent time together while I was traveling. I don't think anyone will question it."

"We'll figure it out as we go along," he said easily. "We just need to be in agreement that if one of us takes the lead on something, the other one will follow. We can't disagree about stuff in front of your family, okay?"

Emma knew he was right. She wasn't all that confident they could convince anyone that they were a couple, but she was grateful Cort was willing to try. It was only for three days, after all. "Thank you. I appreciate you giving up your weekend to do this for me."

He flashed her a swift grin, revealing a charming indent in one cheek. "Well, I do have an ulterior motive. When I found out the wedding was in Last Stand, I signed up for a bull riding event in town on the Fourth of July."

Emma gaped at him. "In Last Stand?"

"Yes, ma'am. It's not an official PBR event, but Trent Campbell is the master of ceremonies." He grinned as Emma stared blankly at him. "He's a former PBR star. The event draws a good crowd and the prize money isn't bad."

Emma stared at him in dismay. "No, you can't do this."

"Excuse me?"

Emma saw the glint in his eyes, and how his jaw flexed, but ignored it. "Don't you see? The rodeo isn't for another two weeks...and if you stay here, then my family will expect me to stay too."

"And that's a bad thing?"

He didn't understand. How could he? Staying in Last Stand for even one day longer than necessary would cause her all kinds of hell with her mother. "I promised I would be back to work on Tuesday," she said lamely.

"Can't you arrange it with your boss? It's your mom, right? I thought that's what you told me on the phone last week." He glanced at her. "If we're as in love as you want your family to believe, they'd think it strange if you decided to go back to New York, and leave me here."

He was right.

But as the truck roared north, Emma's stomach churned with the weight of the lies she had willingly agreed to tell her family. And the biggest lie of all was that she wasn't attracted to the man beside her.

Chapter Five

A S THEY DREW closer to the Last Stand town limits, Cort sensed Emmaline's increasing anxiety. She shifted in her seat, periodically drawing in deep, calming breaths and blowing them out slowly. He didn't think she was even aware she did it. He wanted to offer some comfort, but no way was he going to touch her again. Their one brief contact earlier in the drive had sent a current of awareness through him, and he'd very nearly snatched his hand back. Emmaline hadn't been immune, either. Under different circumstances, he'd have worked that mutual attraction to his advantage, but this was no normal weekend. Emmaline Claiborne had enough stress in her life right now without him piling on.

"Oh, look, it's Rosa's Cantina," Emma exclaimed, pointing to a roadside restaurant.

The Mexican-themed eatery was housed in a warm pink stucco building with clay roof tiles. Surrounding the structure was a large patio strung with hundreds of lights and sporting dozens of colorful umbrellas. Business was brisk, and the nearby parking lot was more than half full of cars. As they drove past, Emma rolled her window down and put her face out, breathing deeply. Cort caught the tantalizing aroma of grilled steak, and his stomach rumbled.

"Would you like to stop?" he asked hopefully.

Emma sat back and put her window up. "Yes. But only because it would delay the inevitable. I wouldn't be able to eat a thing, and I'd only be procrastinating."

"Are you sure?" Cort pressed.

"I'm sure," she said, her tone regretful. "I'll feel better once we reach the house, and get the initial meet-and-greet over with. My father's housekeeper, Rosa-Maria, used to run the cantina. Now her son owns it, but Rosa-Maria uses all the same recipes when she cooks for my father and brothers. If things aren't too crazy, I'll ask her to make us some steak fajitas."

Before long, they were driving through the business district of the town itself. Shops, restaurants, and businesses of all kinds were housed in limestone buildings that looked to have been built during the nineteenth century and were reminiscent of a frontier town. Emma pointed out the various landmarks.

"That's a statue of Asa Fuhrman," she said. "He's the hero of the actual last stand. And that's the library, and that's the saloon where it all went down."

The Last Stand Saloon looked as if it had been time-warped out of the old West, and Cort noted with interest that the stone walls of the building still bore the scars and bullet holes of the famous battle. The whole town, or what he could see of it from Main Street, had a charming, old-fashioned feel to it. In addition to the many shops and restaurants, there were plenty of tourists too. In what appeared to be the historic district, people strolled along the covered sidewalks, peered into storefront windows, or stood conversing in the afternoon sunshine. Cort could understand why generations of Claibornes had decided to stay and make this place their home. It had a small-town, welcoming feel to it.

After several minutes, they were leaving the pretty downtown of Last Stand behind. The road widened, grew more rural, and they passed vineyards and peach orchards, and sunbaked fields where cattle grazed lazily beneath the shade of live oaks. For a short time, they followed the curve of the Pedernales River, running slow and lazy alongside them, before it curved away and vanished behind the hills.

Following Emmaline's directions, Cort turned onto a road that wound its way through outcroppings of pink rock and swathes of meadow brilliant with wildflowers. They turned again, this time down a hard-packed dirt road beneath lush trees, and through an enormous iron gate flanked on either side by a stone wall that was easily eight feet high. In the distance, Cort could see the ranch called Riverrun.

A sprawling, two-story limestone house with an enormous wraparound porch sat on the crest of a gentle rise, surrounded by stands of pecan trees. Outbuildings and barns dotted the property, and cattle grazed on a sun-dappled hillside to the west. At least a dozen pickup trucks and other vehicles were parked on the grass along the length of the driveway, and small clusters of people congregated on the covered porch.

On the wide stretch of meadow behind the house, a river flowed lazily beneath tall trees, and the biggest wedding tent Cort had ever seen was set up near the riverbank. Box trucks and vans were parked on the grass beyond the tent, and dozens of people carried tables, chairs, statuaries, and enormous pots of flowers into the tent. Two cherry pickers maneuvered beneath the trees as the men standing in the baskets hung lights from overhead branches. The scene was one of organized chaos, and Cort cringed to think of the cost associated with such extravagance.

"Well, this is it," Emmaline said, drawing in a deep breath, her gaze lingering for a long moment on the wedding tent. "There's no turning back now."

Cort parked the truck and killed the engine. Turning in his seat, he looked at Emma. He could read the anxiety on her face, sense her apprehension. "I'll be right beside you," he assured her. "Remember, you're not doing this alone."

Emmaline pulled her gaze from the house and looked at him. For a moment, Cort thought he saw something like longing in her eyes. Then she drew a deep breath and nodded. "Thank you. That means a lot to me."

Climbing out of the truck, Cort came around to her side and opened the door, offering his hand to her. As she slid from the seat, he couldn't help but admire the slender length of her legs encased in the tight pants. When she reached back into the cab for her handbag, her loose blouse gaped away, leaving him with an unobstructed view down the front of her shirt. The underlying tank top did little to conceal the rounded mounds of her breasts, and Cort had an unbidden image of how they would look in his hands. With a stifled groan, he shifted his attention away, focusing instead on the distant cattle.

When she had hitched her tote bag over her shoulder, she turned toward the gravel driveway, tottering in her heels so that Cort put a hand beneath her elbow to steady her. The soft strains of country music drifted toward them from the house, almost drowned out by the persistent buzzing of cicadas in the surrounding trees.

"Doing okay?" he asked.

"So far," she said, picking her way over the uneven ground. "But the day is still young. I can't believe I'm so nervous. I feel like I'm going to the gallows, not a wedding."

"Like I said before," Cort murmured, glancing at the clusters of people on the porch, "you're not alone in this. Use me however you need to, okay? That's why you brought me along."

Emmaline made an incoherent sound and stumbled. She would have gone down, but Cort caught her, hauling her upright until she was pressed against his chest and staring at him with those wide, dark eyes. Her cheeks were flushed and she looked a little dazed. Her gaze dropped to his mouth, and stayed there.

"My heel got caught," she said lamely, her eyes still fixated on his lips. "Must have been some loose gravel…"

Cort bent his head and kissed her.

Emmaline stiffened in his arms for just an instant before going soft and pliant, leaning into him and responding so sweetly that Cort found himself momentarily in danger of forgetting where they were. Which, considering her father and brothers were likely on that porch watching them, wasn't too bright. Reluctantly, he broke the kiss but didn't release her. As kisses went, it had been pretty chaste, but Cort could still taste her, still feel the pillowy softness of her lips. Now he felt the moist heat of her breath against his neck as she spoke.

"Oh. I wondered…"

Her words trailed off.

Cort dipped his head to look into her eyes. "What? What did you wonder?"

He watched as a flush of color stained her neck and crept into her face. "Nothing."

She stepped back, and Cort shoved his hands into his pockets to prevent himself from reaching for her again. He noted with satisfaction that she seemed flustered, and she wouldn't meet his eyes. Instead, she hitched her tote bag higher on her shoulder and gestured vaguely toward the house. "Well, I guess we've let everyone know we're a couple, so that's a good thing."

As they walked across the grass toward the house, Cort reached out and took her hand. After the kiss, holding her hand seemed like a natural thing to do. He told himself he was only doing it to make sure they did look like a couple to those watching, but he knew it was just an excuse.

He wanted to touch her. *He liked touching her.*

He felt her surprise, but she didn't pull away. A man separated himself from a small group and made his way to the wide porch steps. He looked to be in his early sixties, with a shock of silver hair and startling blue eyes in a warm, tanned face. He wasn't a tall man, but even from a distance, he exuded an air of command and there was a glow of enthusiasm about him, as if he woke each morning relishing the thought of whatever life might throw at him. He wore a black snap-front shirt paired with crisp black jeans and boots. Now he came down the steps, and his face creased into a smile as he opened his arms to Emmaline.

"Welcome home, darlin'."

Dropping Cort's hand, Emma stepped into her father's embrace. "Daddy."

Over her head, Gus Claiborne met Cort's eyes, and Cort suddenly had the sense that the older man knew exactly why he was there. Those shrewd eyes reminded him of his granddad, and Cort resisted the urge to fidget beneath that discerning gaze. After a moment, Gus kissed Emma's cheek and murmured something into her ear before releasing her, and extending his hand to Cort. His grip was firm and strong.

"Gus Claiborne," he said. "Welcome to Riverrun."

"Cort Channing. Thank you, sir."

"Call me Gus." He put an arm around Emmaline and hugged her against his side. "I appreciate you being here, Cort. I expect you know this is a difficult weekend for my Emma."

"Less difficult, I hope, with me here," Cort said smoothly.

"Daddy, that's all in the past," Emma interjected, pulling away from her father, and sliding her arm through Cort's.

SWIPE RIGHT FOR A COWBOY

"Everything happens for a reason, and that became clear to me after I met Cort. I was never meant to be with Damon, but it took meeting Cort to show me that."

Gus gave a brief smile, but Cort thought it didn't quite reach his eyes. "I'm happy to hear it. And when did you two meet, exactly?"

"I was in New York about eight months ago," Cort replied. "We met through a mutual friend, and something just clicked."

The fib slid easily off his tongue, and Cort realized it was no less than the truth, at least for his part. From the moment he first saw Emmaline's photo on her dating app profile, he knew he had to meet her. But he wasn't sure Gus was fooled. Emma's father continued to watch them with a certain speculation in his eyes. Thankfully, he didn't pursue the issue. "Well, that's good to hear," Gus said. "Come up to the house and meet the rest of the family, Cort."

"Those are my brothers there," Emma murmured as they fell into step behind her father. "Well, two of them, anyway."

Cort followed her gaze to the two men who stood waiting near the top step, watching their approach. One brother leaned nonchalantly against a support post, arms crossed, while the other bent forward with his forearms resting on the porch railing, fingers casually laced together, but there was nothing casual in the way either man watched their approach. Like their father, they both wore snap-front shirts and jeans, and they both had the same astonishing blue eyes. They straightened as Cort and Emma climbed the steps.

KAREN FOLEY

"Hey, sweetheart," the first man said, and enfolded Emma in a bear hug, nearly lifting her off her feet. "Welcome home. It's good to see you."

"You, too, Evan," Emma said, smiling broadly.

"Hey, kiddo." The second brother came around and pulled Emma in for a swift hug. "How was your flight?"

"Good," she assured him. She pulled Cort forward. "This is my...boyfriend. Cort, I'd like you to meet my brothers, Holt and Evan."

Boyfriend.

It took a second for Cort to understand she was talking about *him*. Shit just got real. Had her father or brothers picked up on the way she'd hesitated before she'd said the word *boyfriend*? As Cort shook hands with both men, they watched him with the same narrowed intensity that Gus had, not exactly unfriendly but not overly welcoming, either. Cort became aware they were drawing curious glances from the other guests who lingered on the covered porch, as they realized who Emma was. Cort suspected their interest now was nothing compared to what it would be when Emma's sister arrived.

"Good to meet you both," he said to her brothers.

"How'd you all meet?" asked the taller brother, Holt. His tone was more suspicious than curious.

"Oh, for God's sake," Emma exclaimed.

"What?" Holt rounded his eyes in a look of innocent surprise.

"Don't pretend you're not giving us the third degree," she said. "We met in New York about eight months ago,

76

through friends."

Evan gave Cort an all-encompassing glance, clearly confused. "I didn't take you for a city boy."

"I'm not," Cort replied. "Texas born and raised, just south of here, actually. I was in New York visiting a friend, and he introduced me to Emmaline. We've pretty much been together since."

Now all three Claiborne men looked at him with renewed interest.

"Where's home for you?" Evan asked.

"I grew up on a ranch in Bandera."

"You'll regret sharing that bit of information." Evan grinned. "Dad'll have you wrangling livestock and mucking out stalls if he thinks you know your way around a ranch."

"I wouldn't mind," Colt said, taking an immediate liking to Evan. He had an open face and a friendly warmth that was engaging.

"What's the last name?" This was from Holt, whose vibe was definitely less pleasant.

"Channing."

"Channing, Channing," Holt said thoughtfully. "Have we met before?"

"Not that I recall."

"The name sounds familiar," Holt murmured, his eyes narrowing as he studied Cort.

"Holt would love to discover that you two somehow know each other," Emma said. "He knows everyone within a hundred-mile radius of Last Stand, and he'd figure out some way to take credit for us being together. In fact, he'd never let me live it down."

Cort kept his features carefully schooled, knowing it was only a matter of time before Holt put two and two together. He should just come clean and tell everyone—Emma included—that his grandfather was none other than Hank Walker, the former breeder of the most famous bucking bulls to enter the arena in the past forty years. But he wasn't ready to play that card yet. People in Hill Country had long memories, and he didn't want to answer the slew of questions he'd get if any of the Claibornes knew of the relationship. He still had something to prove. Maybe winning a championship belt wouldn't convince everyone that he was cut from a different cloth than his father, but it would go a long way toward showing the world he could succeed on his own merit. He didn't need any handouts, thank you very much, and he certainly didn't need to con anyone into giving him what he wanted.

"It may take me a while," Holt murmured, eyeballing Cort with a mixture of suspicion and speculation, "but it'll come to me."

"Pardon our surprise," Evan said, rubbing his chin with one hand as he smiled, "but Emma always swore she'd never date a cowboy." He slanted an amused look toward his sister. "Or let anyone call her Emmaline."

"Well, that's love for you," Emma said brightly, and turned an adoring gaze on Cort, her eyes as soft and dark as a doe's. "It makes a person do things they never thought they were capable of."

Even knowing her sudden adoration was only an act for

her family's benefit, Cort couldn't prevent the heat that gathered beneath his clothes, or the way his pulse reacted, working in hard thumps. He could have sworn Gus Claiborne snorted, but then quickly covered it with a cough.

"My apologies. Pollen season around here can be a killer on the sinuses," he said.

"Speaking of love," Emma said sweetly, "where's the bride?"

"Her bridesmaids took her into town for a surprise afternoon at the spa," came the reply from behind them. "They should be back anytime."

Cort didn't miss how Emma's expression froze, before she turned around with a smile pasted on her lips. "Hello, Damon."

A man stood at the bottom of the porch, one foot on the lowest step. He looked as out of place on the Claiborne ranch as a freshly plucked flower on a shovel of cow manure. *This* was Damon Stewart, the man who'd dumped Emmaline in favor of her sister? Now it was Cort's turn to disguise his own snort behind a sudden cough. The other man was good-looking in a distinctly East Coast way, with his multicolored madras shorts, button-down cotton shirt, and a deep pink pullover sweater tied loosely around his shoulders. His dark hair had some kind of gel in it that kept it sleekly in place, despite the breeze that stirred the wildflowers growing along the driveway. If Cort hadn't already known the guy was a bestselling author of crime fiction, he would have thought he spent his days on the deck of a yacht.

"Emma," Damon said, and climbed the stairs to join

them. "I'm glad you came."

Emma moved closer to Cort until her arm was pressed against his. "I wouldn't miss it." Her voice was cool. "This is still my family and despite everything that's happened, Callie is still my sister."

"I'm relieved to hear it. I hope you can think of me as your brother," Damon said with a smarmy smile.

"I don't think so," Emma replied, her voice cool. "I already have three brothers, and you're not even in the same league."

Gus chuckled, but didn't rebuke his daughter, while Evan laughed outright.

"Ouch," Damon said. "I guess I deserved that."

"Evan," Gus interrupted, still smiling, "why don't you help Cort with the luggage? Emmaline, you'll be in your old room, and I've put Cort in the bunkhouse with some of the other bachelors. Freshen up, and then join us for drinks on the terrace."

"The bunkhouse, Daddy? Really? We're *a couple.*"

Gus stopped and pinioned her with a sharp look. "I wouldn't presume to speculate on the nature of your relationship." He paused. "Normally, I would insist on separate sleeping quarters, but I guess I gave up any right to tell you what to do a long time ago."

Emma gave him a tolerant look. "Daddy, I would never disrespect you, but—"

Gus held up one hand, silencing her. "You're both consenting adults, so I'll leave the sleeping arrangements to you. I may be old, but I know the world is changing. Don't worry; I won't be getting my shotgun out and demanding Cort make an honest woman of you."

"*Daddy.*"

"Honey, I don't mind bunking with the guys," Cort murmured. "This is your father's house, and I respect that."

Emma looked at him, and Cort was struck by the steely resolve in her eyes.

"We stay together," she said simply, but then she turned and looked pointedly at Damon. Cort didn't miss the defiance and challenge in her eyes. She was only doing this to prove a point, and to get under Damon's skin. She had no real desire to share a bedroom or anything else with Cort, but she was willing to sacrifice her principles in order to show Damon that he no longer mattered to her.

Even if it wasn't true.

Chapter Six

"YOU WANT ME to sleep here with you for the next three nights?"

Cort sounded appalled.

Emma dumped her tote bag on the bed in her childhood bedroom and briefly closed her eyes. She was such an idiot! But seeing Damon again had awakened the old anger inside her; the same anger and bitterness that had consumed her in the days and weeks following their abrupt breakup. Seeing him again, she had wanted to do something—*anything*—to wipe the smug smirk off his face.

She'd succeeded.

The flash of disbelief and dismay she'd seen in his eyes as he'd realized that she had moved on and had found someone else to share her life—and her bed—had been totally worth the falsehood. At least, until she heard the aversion in Cort's voice as he set their bags down on the floor and looked around the room they would share.

She turned to face him, and then abruptly lost any ability to speak. Cort had removed his hat and placed it on a pretty gray slipper chair near the door, and now he stood looking at her with an expression that made her toes curl inside her boots, and a shiver of awareness tickle along her spine. Her bedroom was spacious and airy, but all the oxygen seemed to have suddenly been sucked out of the room. Emma could barely breathe. Cort seemed bigger, rougher, and more masculine than usual. That, combined with the way he was looking at her—as if he wanted to consume her—made her legs feel rubbery. She quickly sat down on the edge of the bed.

"What's wrong?" Her voice came out as little more than a squeak.

"You sure this is a good idea?" he asked. His voice was low and gravelly, and scraped across her heightened senses like the rasp of a kitten's tongue.

Emma swallowed. "What do you mean?"

He laughed softly and his sea-green eyes lingered on her for a moment. "Oh, no…you're not going to pretend you have no idea what I'm talking about." He gestured around her bedroom. "Darlin', I'm not sure I can stay in this room with you, and not feel like a complete perv. This looks like a damn honeymoon suite."

In the space of mere hours, she had gone from being called *ma'am* to *honey* and *darlin'*. She wished she didn't like the way it sounded so much. With her heart thumping in her chest, she looked around at their surroundings. She had always preferred a clean, simple look in her décor, and her bedroom was a mixture of dark wood tones, and sumptuous swathes of white organza and silk set against the backdrop of the limestone walls. The windows were open and a soft breeze stirred the floor-length sheers, billowing them into the room in a graceful swirl of gauzy fabric. The bed itself was a large farmhouse-style four-poster, with a ruched white comforter and heaps of pillows. She'd draped a length of sheer white organdy cotton over the canopy frame so that it created an intimate, light-filtering enclosure near the headboard. Someone, probably Rosa-Maria, had placed several small bouquets of wildflowers in the room, one on the bedside table and another on her dresser.

When Emma had redecorated the room during her last visit several years earlier, she'd gone for a serene, timeless look, knowing the room would likely serve as a guest room in her absence. She'd packed away all her childhood treasures and mementos, certain at the time that she'd rarely return to Last Stand. Aside from a cluster of framed photos on top of the dresser, she'd deliberately kept the room from being too personal. Now, seeing it through Cort's eyes, she realized the bedroom was overtly soft and feminine.

Romantic.

Heat washed over Emma, and her heart worked in swift, painful beats. She desperately wanted to change her mind about having him stay in the same room with her. He probably thought she had designs on him, and this was her way of getting into his Wranglers. Not that the thought hadn't occurred to her somewhere between seeing him in his underwear and Last Stand, but she honestly hadn't been thinking straight when she'd all but ordered him to sleep in her bedroom. Because if she had, she would have realized what a colossal mistake it had been to think she could share such intimate space with a man like Cort Channing, and not spend every second of that time thinking about what it might be like to have sex with him.

She blamed him, of course.

If he hadn't kissed her earlier and proved all her fantasies about his luscious mouth were actually true, she might have been able to think of him as a friend. But now it was too late. Now she knew the silky heat of his lips, and the way his mouth moved against hers, searching and slow. The kiss had been over almost before it began, but it had been enough to set Emma's imagination on fire. And certain parts of her anatomy, as well. The realization that she would now have to spend the next three nights in close proximity to him was almost too much to contemplate.

"Listen," she said earnestly, "I'm sorry I put you on the spot like that and said we would share a room." She hesitated. "I had no right to do that. Of course, you should stay in the bunkhouse with the other guys." She chewed her lower lip. "If you want to."

"This is your weekend. I'm just along for the ride, so I'll do whatever you want." His steady gaze never wavered. "Besides, what will your family—and your ex—think about you changing your mind and asking me to sleep in the bunkhouse now?"

They'd likely think she and Cort had had a fight about Damon. "They won't think anything," she assured him. "They'll be too focused on the wedding to even give us a second thought."

"I don't think your father or your brothers miss much," he said slowly. "And trust me when I say your ex is going to know if I suddenly decide to pull up stakes and move my camp to the bunkhouse. You said your preference is for us to look like a real couple. *Like two people who are in love,* maybe."

Emma groaned and curled her fingers into the bedding. "I also said we wouldn't be sharing a room, and yet here we are."

"I'd say it's not too late to change your mind," Cort said, his tone careful, "but I'm pretty sure that bull has left the chute. Having me sleep in the bunkhouse isn't going to send the message you want."

"Damon is marrying *my sister* in two days," she retorted. "Why should he even care?"

"Trust me, honey," Cort drawled. "He cares. He's a dog in the manger if I ever saw one, and even though he's made his choice, it stands to reason a guy like him has a big ego. He'd enjoy knowing we're not sleeping together, especially if he believes he's the reason why."

Cort was right. Damon would laugh all the way down the aisle. But she honestly didn't know if she could share a room with a drop dead gorgeous, sexy cowboy like Cort Channing. That scenario just begged for trouble, because she was feeling both vulnerable and vengeful, and he represented everything she swore she had no interest in.

"I'll tell you what," Cort said. His voice was quiet and calm, as if she was a wild mare he was afraid of spooking. "I'll sleep on the floor. You're safe with me, Emmaline. I agreed to play the part of your boyfriend for the weekend, and if sharing a room will help you hold your head high, then I'm game."

Much to her shame, Emma had hoped he would say something to that effect. Call her naïve, but she believed he really would sleep on the floor, because he was that unique brand of Texan who had been raised to respect women, and to love God, his country, and his momma, and not necessarily in that order. And maybe if she took sleeping pills and wore a sleep mask and earplugs, she could let him sleep on the floor. She wouldn't lie awake and wonder what he wore to bed, or if he made any noises when he dreamt, or if his face looked younger in sleep. Nope. Definitely not.

"Okay, deal," she said before she could change her mind.

Cort pulled her to her feet, lacing his fingers with hers. "You're going to get through this. C'mon, let me see your game face."

His consideration and attention still did funny things to her insides, and she wasn't sure he was aware that he was also using his thumbs to stroke her hands where they were joined. She could feel the hard calluses against her skin, distracting her and making it difficult to focus on his words. Somehow, she managed a smile.

Cort grinned. "No, that's definitely not going to work. Are you sure you're okay? You look like you're coming down with something."

Emma *felt* as if she was coming down with something. She felt hot one second and shivery the next, with no ability to concentrate on anything except that decadent mouth, smiling at her now as if it knew exactly what it was doing to her.

Dragging her gaze from Cort's lips, she looked him in the eyes and drew in a deep breath. "I'm fine, just a little worn out from the flight."

A knock at the door prevented Cort from replying, and then Rosa-Maria poked her head in, her dark eyes smiling. "*Hola*, Emmaline," she said, her arms filled with bath towels.

"Rosa!" Emma took the towels from the older woman, and gave her a swift hug, kissing her cheek. "It's so good to see you!"

Rosa-Maria had been her father's housekeeper and cook for as long as Emma could remember. She'd also managed to keep the Claiborne brood in line when they were young, and had acted as a surrogate mother to Emma when she'd visited the ranch as a child. Rosa-Maria had always been a warm, stabilizing presence in the male-dominated household, and Emma had fond memories of "helping" in the kitchen when she was very young. Rosa was as much a part of the Claiborne family as Emma was, maybe even more so.

"It is good to see you too," the older woman said. "And who is this handsome young man?"

"This is my—"

"Cort Channing, ma'am," Cort said, stepping forward to shake Rosa-Maria's hand. "I hope I'm not causing you additional work by staying in the main house with Emma-line."

He gave Rosa-Maria a smile that would have melted the panties off a younger woman, and Emma could see the housekeeper was completely charmed. For a moment, she looked almost girlish and Emma realized with surprise that

Rosa-Maria was still a beautiful woman. Her long, black hair was pulled back in a tidy bun, with only a hint of gray at her temples. Her brown skin was smooth, and the only wrinkles were the laugh lines at the corners of her dark eyes.

"Of course not," Rosa-Maria said, smiling broadly. "If my Emmaline is happy, then my heart is happy. If you need anything, please let me know."

"Are there any formal plans for tonight?" Emma asked. "I haven't had a chance to talk to Daddy about the schedule for this weekend."

Emma knew she didn't misread the sympathy that flashed in Rosa's eyes. "We have a full house tonight," she said, "but nothing too formal. Drinks and finger foods are being served now on the terrace, and Jessie is serving a buffet dinner for everyone at eight o'clock."

Emma grinned. Jessie was Rosa's granddaughter. Together with her father, she ran the Montero family restaurant on the outskirts of Last Stand.

"Cort, didn't I promise you a steak fajita from Rosa's Cantina?" She looked back at Rosa. "We passed the cantina coming into town, and it smelled amazing. Cort wanted to stop, but I made him keep driving."

Rosa beamed at Cort. "We're doing a Mexican buffet, so you can try a little of everything."

"I'm looking forward to it."

"Come downstairs when you're ready," she said to Emma. "Your father and brothers are on the patio."

After she left, Emma turned to Cort. "I think you've made a conquest."

"I think with Rosa, it's more a case of *any friend of yours is a friend of mine*."

"She didn't like Damon when I brought him home."

"Maybe she knew he wasn't the right guy for you."

Emma couldn't prevent a flash of annoyance. "Why does everyone keep saying that? Why was he not right for me, but he's right for my sister?"

"I can't answer that, since I haven't met your sister."

"No doubt you'll be as charmed by her as everyone else is," Emma muttered darkly.

"Is that what you're worried about, honey? That even your phony boyfriend will prefer your sister to you?"

To Emma's mortification, hot tears stung the backs of her eyes and a hard lump formed in her throat. She shook her head. She couldn't have formed words right then if her life depended on it, because Cort had guessed her dark secret—that she would never be quite good enough. She'd known it for most of her life, since she'd been a small girl and her mother had taken her away from her father and brothers, and they hadn't come to New York to bring her home. She hadn't been good enough for her daddy to want her back. Then, when she'd finally gotten her degree in fine arts, her mother had gently told her that her artwork wasn't quite right for the gallery yet. But Emma had understood what she really meant—her work wasn't good enough. *She* wasn't good enough. And then Damon had dumped her in favor of her sister.

Gentle fingers tipped her chin up and through blurred vision, Emma saw Cort's concerned expression. His hand slid to the curve of her cheek, and he used his thumb to brush away a tear that had leaked out and slid down to her chin.

"Don't cry," he said in a gruff voice before he pulled her into his arms, enfolding her in his warm embrace.

Emma kept her hands between them, fisted against his chest, when all she really wanted to do was burrow into his hard, protective body. It had been so long since anyone had touched her or held her. She just wanted to press her hot face against his shoulder and stay like this, breathing in his scent.

"I'm not crying," she protested, but her voice sounded wobbly and unconvincing.

She felt his chest move as he laughed quietly, and his breath puffed against her hair. His voice was a deep, purring drawl, the Texas accent stronger now.

"Liar."

Emma uncurled her hands and flattened them against his chest, intending to push out of his arms, but beneath her palms she could feel the hard, steady thump of his heart and feel the heat of his body seeping through his shirt. Seemingly against her will, her fingers splayed out over the thick muscles of his chest. In the opening of his shirt, a pulse beat strongly at the base of his throat. More than anything, Emma wanted to press her lips against that small throb. Only with the greatest difficulty did she manage to resist. She wasn't crying anymore, but her breathing came in swift, shallow inhales. She was surrounded by his heat and scent, that intoxicating blend of spice and leather that was quickly becoming familiar to her. When she lifted her face, she realized Cort's mouth was just inches from her own, his eyes as fathomless as the East River that flowed past her New York apartment. Right now, they were riveted on her mouth. Emma felt her own mouth open on a wordless *oh*. With a defeated groan, Cort lowered his head.

Any thought of pushing him away was lost beneath a searing blaze of sensation. Cort's mouth was lush, fusing with hers in a slow, thorough kiss that had her opening her lips to allow for the hot slide of his tongue against hers. He made a deep sound of approval and gathered her closer, locking one arm around her hips as he slanted his mouth more firmly over hers. His other hand slid to the back of her head to cradle the nape of her neck and hold her still. He kissed her in a way that Damon never had, as if there was no rush and no need for anything beyond this sensual exploration, as if tasting her was all he'd ever wanted.

But it wasn't enough for Emma. The silken heat of his tongue caused an answering throb of need, and she shifted closer, sliding her hands up over his powerful shoulders to the back of his neck. His skin was hot to the touch, and she stroked the hard muscles there before sifting her fingers through his short hair, reveling in the cool silkiness of the heavy layers. Her touch seemed to unleash something in Cort, and he kissed her longer, deeper, his mouth turning more demanding. Emma welcomed the insistent intrusion of his tongue, trying to draw him in farther. His hands slid down her back until they cupped her rear, lifting her so that she felt his arousal, hard and unrelenting, against her hip.

Emma melted against him, wanting more. The throbbing had turned into a persistent, pulsing ache, a need to be filled and taken. How long had it been since she'd had sex? Since she'd even wanted sex? During the last few months she'd lived with Damon, they had rarely been intimate. He'd always claimed he was too tired, or that she was too demanding. He'd made her feel ashamed for wanting sex. But with Cort, she felt that whatever she wanted—whatever she *needed*—he would willingly give it to her, and more. She just needed to tell him.

She broke the kiss, panting. "Cort—"

"Shh, honey," he whispered, and used his mouth to tease the sensitive skin beneath her ear, before slowly working his way along the length of her neck, nibbling and biting gently. "Let me."

Emma shivered and trembled, arching against him and tilting her head to give him better access. Cort's hands still cupped her bottom, and now he inserted a knee between her legs and pulled her closer, until she found herself riding the hard muscle of this thigh. The friction only fueled her rising desire, and she sighed with pleasure and pressed closer, rubbing shamelessly against him. They fit together well, her hips perfectly aligned with his, her head pressed against his shoulder as he worked his mouth over her throat.

A burst of laughter and snatches of conversation drifted through the open window from the patio below, and Emma caught the words *jealous* and *sibling rivalry* before the voices were drowned out in more laughter. She told herself the words could have been used in any context. There was no reason to think someone had used them in reference to herself, but it was too late. She felt as if she'd been dashed with a bucket of ice water.

She pushed against Cort's arms and he released her immediately. A flush of color rode across his cheekbones and the bridge of his nose, and his eyes were still hot with need, but Emma could see that he had heard the conversation too.

"Darlin', don't pay any attention—"

"This is why I didn't want to come," she said hoarsely. She wrapped her arms around her middle. "Everyone thinks I'm only here to ruin Callie's special day. They think I'm jealous, that I want him back."

"Are you still in love with him?" Cort's voice was quiet.

Was she? Seeing Damon again had stirred up all kinds of feelings, none of which she was willing to explore too closely. Her current feelings about Damon—anger and resentment—were all jumbled up with the memories she carried from when they had been a couple. Had she been happy then? She no longer remembered.

"I don't know," she whispered, miserable.

Cort blew out a hard breath and scrubbed a hand over his face before looking at her with something like resignation in his eyes. Seeing her distress, his face softened. "Hey, come here."

Emma offered no resistance when he pulled her back into his arms. But there was nothing sexual about this embrace. It was meant as comfort and support.

"I'm sorry," she said.

"Nothing to be sorry for," he assured her. "That guy is an ass, and your family expects too much if they think you can smile your way through the wedding." He paused. "The real crime is that he's going to become part of your family and, like it or not, you're going to have deal with him for the rest of your life."

"I don't think I'll be back in Texas anytime soon," she admitted, "so I don't see that as a problem."

"What about holidays, birthdays…more weddings? Your brothers are bound to get married one day."

Emma pulled out of his sheltering arms. "I doubt my family would even notice if I wasn't there."

"C'mon, you don't really believe that."

"It's true." Emma's voice was glum, but she was feeling particularly self-pitying at that moment. "I may be a Claiborne, but I've never really been part of the family. My mother took me to New York when I was just three, so my participation in family events has always been sporadic, at best."

"Families aren't always neat and tidy. They're complex and messy and confusing as all hell, but that doesn't mean they don't love you. But it's a two-way street, darlin'. You have to make the effort."

Something in his voice made Emma look sharply at him. Had Cort made an effort with his grandfather? She longed to ask what had happened to his parents, and why his relationship with his grandfather had been strained, but his expression was shuttered and she was too much of a coward to probe. Strains of music drifted through the open window, reminding her that a celebration was underway.

"We should probably go downstairs before someone gets

the wrong idea," she said, even as a part of her acknowledged she would be happier hiding out in her bedroom. She had no desire to mingle and socialize with anyone.

A smile quirked Cort's mouth and his gaze moved over her face. "Or maybe the right idea. You look as if you've just had a good romp."

Glancing in the mirror over her dresser, Emma realized he was right. Her lips were kiss-swollen and the side of her neck was reddened where his stubble had chafed the sensitive skin.

"I should splash some cool water on my face," she murmured, but as she turned toward the adjacent bathroom, Cort caught her gently by the wrist.

"No, leave it." His free hand lifted to her face, stroking her cheek with the backs of his fingers. "It's a good look on you."

There was a masculine satisfaction in his expression, and a sort of possessiveness that should have alarmed Emma, but instead filled her with a secret thrill of excitement. As she followed him out of the bedroom and downstairs, she wondered just how far she might be willing to go with this man, and if her reasons had anything to do with making Damon jealous, or if they came from somewhere much deeper and more personal.

Chapter Seven

EVEN BEFORE SHE saw the wide, double French doors that led onto the terrace, Emma heard the mingled lilt of voices and laughter, the clink of glassware, and the soft strains of country music. She pulled Cort to a stop in the hallway outside her father's office. The door to that private domain, which had been strictly off-limits to her as a child, was tightly closed. From behind the door, Emma heard the distinct tone of masculine voices, although she couldn't make out the words themselves. It shouldn't have surprised her that even on the weekend of his daughter's wedding, Gus Claiborne couldn't put his business dealings aside. She would have liked his solid presence beside her when she finally saw Callie again.

"I don't think I can do this."

"Sure you can, honey," Cort said, his eyes warm as he surveyed her anxious face. "I'll be right beside you."

"People are going to stare at me."

"Damn right they are," he murmured. "You're a beautiful woman."

His words gave her some courage, even if he'd only meant them as a means to boost her confidence. "Don't leave me alone," she begged, and reached blindly for his hand.

"Not a chance."

Taking her hand firmly in his, he led her through to the kitchen, where Rosa-Maria and an attractive young woman were unloading large covered food containers from a wheeled cart to a center island. Seeing them, Rosa-Maria smiled.

"Emmaline, you remember Jessie?" She pulled the other woman forward with a proud smile. "She runs the cantina with her father now, but she always comes to help me when I need her. I don't know what I would do without her, my good girl."

Emma remembered Jessie from when they were both children. Jessie was two years younger and had pretty much lived at the ranch whenever Emma had come to visit. Emma remembered her as a slight brown-skinned girl with a wild mane of black hair and endless amounts of energy. The two of them had gotten into their share of mischief over the years, until Emma's visits had grown more and more infrequent and the friendship had eventually petered out. Emma hadn't been surprised to hear Callie and Jessie had become friendly in her absence, since they were even closer in age.

But this young woman bore little resemblance to the laughing, exuberant child that Emma remembered from her youth. Jessie Montero had grown up. She was gorgeous, with warm, glowing skin and lustrous, dark hair highlighted with ribbons of caramel and copper. She'd always been petite, but now she was taller than Emma, and curvy in all the right places.

"Emma!" she said, smiling with pleasure. Wiping her

hands on the seat of her jeans, she came around the corner of the island and held out her arms. "Look at you! You are stunning!"

Something loosened in Emma's chest, and she realized she had been holding her breath, certain that Jessie would rebuff her now that she was Callie's friend. But the younger woman threw her arms around Emma and hugged her with a fierceness that belied her slender frame.

"I've missed you!" she said, and planted a kiss on Emma's cheek. Then, lowering her voice, she spoke directly into Emma's ear, too low for anyone else to hear. "I'm sorry for what you're going through. We'll talk later, okay?"

Emma nodded, and when they pulled apart, she indicated the man who stood silently beside her. "This is Cort Channing, my boyfriend."

"My pleasure," Cort said. He cast a meaningful look at the food trays. "I hope I can hold out until the buffet is served. Your steak fajitas smell pretty damn good."

Jessie laughed. "I think I can spare one or two now, if you're hungry."

"If I were you, I'd go for the carne asada."

The deep voice came from behind them, and Emma turned to see Holt standing in the doorway of the kitchen, his blue eyes gleaming. Now he surveyed the food dishes with anticipation.

"That's always been your favorite," Emma remarked, "ever since I can remember. Don't you ever want something different?"

"Why mess with perfection?" He lifted back a corner of

aluminum foil on one chafing dish to steal a bit of thinly sliced steak. Rosa-Maria slapped his hand, but he grinned unrepentedly and ate it with relish. "Delicious."

Suddenly quiet, Jessie retreated behind the island and busied herself putting together several fajitas for Cort, tossing steak and vegetables onto a hot skillet to heat them through. But Emma didn't miss how her gaze flicked repeatedly to Holt. She seemed drawn to Emma's oldest brother. Holt, for his part, never even glanced at Jessie. She might have been invisible for all the interest he took in her, which Emma found even more fascinating, considering Jessie was both pretty and vivacious.

Now Holt shifted his attention to Emma, and his expression grew serious. "How are you doing, sweetheart?"

For as long as Emma could recall, Holt had always looked out for her. He'd been her protector when the twins had tormented her, or when she'd managed to get herself into trouble with her father. With nearly eight years between them, she had hero-worshipped him and followed him everywhere on the ranch, and he'd rarely complained. He'd left for college when Emma turned ten, and Riverrun had lost some of its magic in his absence. She'd been sixteen when he'd gotten married. She had been too young and had lived too far away to understand what he'd gone through when his marriage had failed just four years later, and his wife had dragged him through the courts for a very public, very ugly divorce. Emma only knew that following the divorce, he'd thrown himself into his work with a single-minded fervor. He'd changed too. He'd become solemn and even a bit aloof. If he'd dated anyone seriously in the seven years since, he'd been discreet about it. Emma had never heard so much as a whisper about any romantic involvements.

"I'm doing fine," she reassured him, but couldn't prevent her gaze from sliding to Cort, who had moved to the other side of the kitchen. He chatted easily with Jessie as she cooked, but Emma knew he was trying to give her and Holt some privacy. She watched as Jessie handed him a plate heaped with food, and he tucked into it with gusto, leaning against the counter and making appreciative noises as he ate, much to Jessie's amusement.

"I thought you should know that Callie has returned," Holt said quietly. "She's on the terrace. I just didn't want you to be blindsided."

Emma looked at her brother in surprise. "You almost sound like you're on my side."

"There are no sides," he said evenly. "You're both my sisters, and I love you equally. But I don't agree with someone finding their own happiness at someone else's expense, and when that someone else is your own sister…"

Emma felt a rush of gratitude toward Holt. Since they'd announced their engagement, she'd very nearly convinced herself that everyone in the family supported Callie's decision, and that she was the one overreacting. She hadn't seen her sister in almost a year and although she'd tried many times to imagine what it would be like when they finally crossed paths again, she found she wasn't prepared.

"My heart is pounding so hard, I think I'm going to pass

out," she confessed in a shaky voice. "I thought I'd accepted what happened, but now that I'm here—"

"I think she's even more nervous than you are," Holt said. "This hasn't been all rainbows and roses for her, either, especially since Dad made it clear he doesn't approve."

That caught Emma's attention. "He said that?"

"He initially refused to host the wedding here on the ranch," Holt said. "He said it would be disrespectful to you. Callie begged him, and even then, he wouldn't budge. Callie threw a fit. Her mother had to finally step in and shame the old man into allowing it. Then he said he wouldn't walk her down the aisle, which just about broke Callie's heart. He relented, but only reluctantly."

Emma knew her younger sister well enough to know that Callie could have foregone all the elegant trappings, the catered food and the live music, as long as the wedding took place on the ranch. In Callie's mind, that was the one thing that would cement her status as a bonafide member of the Claiborne family. That their father would have considered denying her that astounded Emma.

"I can't believe he didn't want her to have her dream wedding," she said in surprise.

"He just didn't want her to have it at your expense."

"Even so, he had to have known she would be crushed," Emma said. "She's had it all planned since she was a teenager, with wedding tents and fairy lights, and a live band playing Frank Sinatra music. She even wanted someone to release two thousand floating candles up river after dark, so that they'd float past the house."

"Well, she got her way in the end."

"She always does," Emma said, knowing she sounded bitter but unable to help herself. "Who's catering?"

"The Hutchinson brothers."

"Oh," Emma said. "Don't they run the barbeque joint in town?"

"They do."

Emma started to laugh. She couldn't help herself.

"What's funny?" asked Holt.

"It's just that Damon is a vegetarian," she explained, covering her mirth with one hand. "I can't believe he agreed to do barbeque for his wedding meal, when one of our worst arguments happened after I cooked a steak in the apartment and all the fire detectors went off! He was furious, and complained that he'd never get rid of the odor!"

"Proof the two of you weren't meant to be together," Holt said with a grin, and hooked an arm around her neck to pull her in for a quick hug. "You can take the girl out of Texas, but you can't take Texas out of the girl. Something tells me you're going to be just fine."

His words caused a warm and hopeful feeling to unfurl and ribbon its way through Emma. Despite having been born in Last Stand, she'd never considered herself a Texas girl. She was a New Yorker, through and through. Hadn't her mother said so innumerable times? But what she'd never told her mother was how much she'd cherished the time she spent in Texas. Here, she could breathe. She could sleep with her windows open, serenaded by the rhythmic sound of the crickets and cicadas, where the warm breezes carried the scent of wildflowers and freshly mown hay, and the only traffic jams were when the locals headed to Kolaches, the German bakery, for breakfast on Sunday morning.

"Thanks," she said, returning her brother's hug before pulling away and drawing in a deep breath. "Well, I guess I can't delay the inevitable. Where is she?"

"She's sitting on the patio with her bridesmaids," Holt said.

Emma looked to where Cort was washing his dish in the sink. As if he sensed her eyes on him, he looked up. For just an instant, there was a glint in those fathomless eyes that caused heat to collect beneath the surface of her skin. A smile curved one side of his mouth, as if he was completely aware of the effect he had on her. Emma gave him a bright smile, thinking about the way his mouth felt pressed against hers, and how hard and warm his chest had been when he'd folded her in his arms. He crossed the kitchen, his eyes never leaving hers.

"You look flushed," he murmured when he reached her side.

"I'm not used to the Texas heat," she lied. "C'mon, I'll introduce you to my sister."

There were at least thirty people on the wide bluestone terrace, laughing and drinking as they clustered around small tables. While not quite dark outside, the sun had settled behind the hills, and the sky had turned a pretty shade of purple and pink. A small group of children ran around on the grass beyond the patio, chasing lightning bugs while one of the ranch dogs romped joyfully beside them. Beneath a webbing of twinkling fairy lights, the terrace looked both romantic and festive.

An expansive bar had been set up close to the French doors, and a young bartender served drinks while two aproned girls passed trays of hot and cold hors d'oeuvres. Enormous urns of flowers made a colorful border around the patio, and Callie sat at a table on one side, surrounded by a half dozen pretty girls. Emma tried not to think about the fact that under different circumstances, she might have been Callie's maid of honor.

A group of men lounged nearby, talking boisterously and laughing at something one of them had said. Emma recognized several of them as friends of Damon, whom she had met once or twice when they had been together. Damon, thank goodness, was nowhere to be seen, but Emma caught sight of Rachel Dean standing with an older couple and holding a champagne flute. Tall and slim, with red hair that hung to her shoulders, she was hard to miss. A few years younger than Emma's mother, Rachel was still an attractive woman. Emma had only met her a couple of times and although the exchanges had always been pleasant, she had no desire to cross paths with her now. For as long as she could recall, Rachel Dean had been characterized by her mother as the devil incarnate; the single reason for the failure of her marriage.

Then Emma's gaze moved to the couple she stood with, and she felt her stomach turn into knots. During the three years she had been with Damon, she'd met his parents at least a dozen times. Worse, she had *liked* them. She should have known they would be here, but seeing them at her father's ranch, smiling and talking with Rachel Dean, caused reality to crash down around her.

"I can't do this," she whispered. "Those are Damon's parents, over there."

"I'm right here," he reassured her. "If you need to leave, I'll make our excuses."

Emma dragged in a deep breath. "No, it's okay. I just didn't think—I wasn't prepared to see them."

"You haven't done anything wrong," he said. "You've got no reason to feel ashamed."

Emma edged closer to Cort and tried to remain as inconspicuous as possible. Even so, she was aware of the attention she drew as she stepped onto the patio. In her black ankle pants and heeled boots, she might as well have had a sign around her neck that read, Not from Around Here. She had a moment of panic, where her heartbeat throbbed in her ears and blackness flickered at the edges of her vision. Even the country music that played through unseen speakers faded from her hearing.

"I think I'm going to pass out," she breathed, at the same instant Cort's arm came around her, supporting her and drawing her a little away from the people.

"When's the last time you ate?"

Emma couldn't recall. She'd had an obnoxiously early flight out of New York that morning, had changed planes in Chicago, and had been too anxious to even think about eating anything on the flight. She made no objection when Cort intercepted one of the serving girls and snagged two small hors d'oevres from her tray.

"Here, eat this," he said, and while Emma obediently ate the two blinis topped with smoked salmon and crème fraiche, he stepped over to the bar. He returned less than a minute later with a glass of juice. "Drink. Your blood sugar is probably low, which is why you feel faint. You'll be better in a minute."

"Thank you," she said when she had finished and he had set her glass on a nearby tray. "I'm better now."

"You need something more substantial," he said, concern clouding his eyes. He began to turn away, his eyes searching the food trays, but Emma put a restraining hand on his arm.

"Cort, I'm fine." She smiled at him, appreciating his care. "Really."

His eyes flickered over in a swift appraisal. "Okay, but if you feel unwell, just tell me and we can go somewhere quiet." He frowned. "I thought Rosa-Maria said this wasn't a formal affair tonight."

Emma glanced around and grimaced. "This is informal, at least for my sister. The real show will be the wedding reception. Callie has always wanted a big wedding. We should go say hello to her before it becomes awkward."

"Sweetheart, where I come from, it got awkward about a year ago," Cort said with a wry grin.

His smile was infectious, and as he led her across the terrace, Emma realized she didn't have to fake her own smile. As they approached the table where Callie sat, people moved aside, clearing a path. Callie's bridesmaids, however, clustered closer to their friend, clearly expecting a confrontation between the sisters. When Emma finally stood on the opposite side of the table, she saw Callie sitting rigidly upright in her chair, her hands folded in her lap and a look of pleasant expectation on her face.

Emma wasn't fooled.

Callie was terrified of an altercation that would ruin her perfect weekend. She looked even prettier than Emma remembered. With her slender frame, long red hair, and abundance of freckles, she was the image of her mother, Rachel Dean. But her dazzling blue eyes were one-hundred percent Claiborne.

"Hello, Emmaline." There was only a trace of nervousness in her voice. "I'm so glad you were able to make it."

"I wouldn't miss this for the world," Emma replied sweetly. "You look beautiful, by the way."

"Thank you." Callie looked expectantly at Cort. "And this handsome gentleman must be your plus-one?"

She referred to the wedding invitation, which had been addressed to Emma, with a plus one next to her name, indicating she could bring a date. "Yes, this is my boyfriend, Cort Channing."

Cort inclined his head in a respectful nod. "Pleased to meet you, ma'am, and congratulations. Emma and I wish you every happiness."

"You're Emma's boyfriend?" Callie managed to infuse a touch of surprised disbelief into her voice, and her bridesmaids tittered nervously.

"Yes, ma'am."

"You sound surprised," Emma commented. She had

been prepared for Callie to be hostile, perhaps due to a sense of guilt over stealing Damon from her, but she hadn't expected this almost mocking attitude.

Callie glanced at her bridesmaids, as if she thought they required an explanation. "Emmaline has always hated coming to the ranch, and she has always disliked cowboys." She gave Cort an appraising look. "Although I can see why you made an exception in this case."

Only Cort's hand at her waist, applying gentle pressure, reminded Emma to be civil. "I don't ever recall saying that I disliked cowboys, and I've never said I hated coming to the ranch," she replied, smiling. "In fact, I've always enjoyed my visits."

"And why wouldn't you? Daddy always rolls out the red carpet for you, and Holt and the twins make it their mission in life to ensure you have a great time." Callie's eyes had a suspicious glitter to them. "Well, I hope you have a great time this weekend, watching me and Damon get hitched."

Emma's heart pounded so painfully, she thought for sure everyone must hear it. She was so stunned by Callie's animosity that for a moment, she couldn't think of a response.

"C'mon, darlin'," Cort said, his voice amiable. "I think Jessie is serving supper. I don't know about you, but I'm hungry. How about we get a bite to eat and go to bed early, hmm? We did say this weekend was going to be our own romantic getaway, didn't we?"

His voice held enough suggestion to be intimate, without being lewd, and Emma was gratified to see Callie blink in surprise. Emma was so grateful for his easy rescue of the situation that she gave him a brilliant smile. "Yes, that sounds perfect. Good night, Callie."

As they made their way back across the patio, Cort's hand was warm and strong at the small of her back. But instead of steering her toward the buffet tables, he led her through the house and toward the front door.

"Where are we going?" she asked.

"Let's step outside and get some fresh air."

"But we just came from outside," Emma said with a breathless laugh.

"That wasn't fresh air, sweetheart," he said with a grim smile. "That was pure jealousy, thick enough to slice."

"What possible reason would Callie have to be jealous?" she asked. "She got what she wanted. She's marrying Damon in two days."

"Honey," Cort drawled, "if you don't know, then I'm not about to tell you."

They were in the hallway now, passing by her father's study when the door suddenly opened and her father stepped out. Lost in his own thoughts, he was unaware of their presence until he almost collided with Emma. He looked surprised to see them.

"Why aren't you both with the other young people, enjoying yourselves?" he asked.

"We are enjoying ourselves, Daddy. The real question is, why are you working?"

"Who says I'm working?" He gave her a quick wink. "I was just going in to help myself to the buffet, and then step outside to sit with our guests."

"Okay, then, we won't stop you. Cort and I are just going for a walk."

"Good, good." Her father seemed preoccupied, and Emma wasn't certain if he had even heard her. He began walking in the direction of the buffet room, and suddenly stopped. "Cort Channing."

"Sir?"

"What did you say your grandfather's name was again?" Gone was the distracted air. His focus on Cort was sharp and intent.

"I didn't, sir."

"No? I could have sworn you said, but I seem to have forgotten."

Emma wasn't fooled. She'd seen that expression on her father's face before. He never forgot anything. He was playing Cort, but Emma couldn't understand why.

"It's not important," Cort said with a shrug. "He passed away almost a year ago. We weren't close."

"I'm sorry to hear that," Gus said. "Well, I won't keep you. Enjoy your walk."

Emma frowned as they watched him walk away. "What was that all about?"

"My guess is he's doing a background check on me, and just wants to confirm my lineage," Cort said, his voice dry.

"He'd do better to run a background check on Damon Stewart," she replied. "At least you're not trying to marry into the family." Cort was quiet, and Emma looked at him in amusement. "You're not, right?"

"I don't know," he replied, his eyes glinting with humor. "Are you rich?"

Emma laughed. "If you have to ask, you aren't from the Hill Country."

"I'll take that as a yes."

"Daddy does just fine, but the real money is on my mother's side of the family," Emma said. "My grandparents said she took a step down when she married my father, and they weren't talking about his DNA."

"How did your parents meet? From what you've told me, they seem an unlikely pair."

Emma shrugged. "Mom was just getting started in the art business, and my father commissioned the gallery she worked at to provide some pieces for the ranch. She came down to do a preliminary evaluation, and I think she fell in love with him. My dad was pretty handsome, and he can charm the rattle off a snake when he puts his mind to it."

"I can see that," Cort acknowledged.

"Well, it didn't take them long to realize they weren't suited. Mom missed the city, but I think she could have been happy if my dad had just paid more attention to her. But he's a workaholic, and she was left alone much of the time with four children, three of whom weren't even hers."

They stepped onto the front porch, and Emma drew in a deep, cleansing breath. The air was warm and humid from the day, and the sounds from the patio were muted enough that she could hear the crickets in the tall grass.

"When you're breeding bucking bulls," Cort offered conversationally as they made their way slowly across the lawn, away from the house, "choosing the right mother becomes all important. If you don't have a good cow, it doesn't matter how exceptional the bull's DNA is."

Emma gave a shout of laughter. "Oh my goodness, did you just call my mother *a cow*?"

Cort chuckled. "No, ma'am. I'm simply acknowledging that when it comes to genetics, moms rule."

Darkness had descended quickly, and in the dense underbrush near the river, dozens of tiny lights blinked off and on. Emma watched the group of children as they chased the lightning bugs with their plastic bug jars.

"How do you know so much about breeding bulls?"

"My granddad was one of the top breeders in the country before I was born." Cort's voice held a measure of pride. "He did it all…artificial insemination, in vitro fertilization, egg collection, and sperm extraction. Some of his bucking bulls were only successfully ridden once or twice during their careers."

Emma knew a little about bull riding and breeding bulls from listening to her brothers. Holt managed the breeding program at the ranch, but had also talked about one day starting a business of his own, breeding bucking bulls.

"What happened to the bulls after your grandfather passed?"

Cort shrugged. "By the time I was old enough to be interested, he'd pretty much sold off his best bulls and was out of the business. By the time I turned eighteen, I was getting more recognition riding in local events, and I couldn't wait to get out on my own and make a name for myself." He shrugged. "I should have paid more attention to what was happening on the ranch, but my granddad made it clear I'd outstayed my welcome, so I left."

"Why? What happened between you? What would make someone turn his back on his grandson?"

"It's a long story," Cort said. "Forget it."

They had reached the edge of the property where the massive wedding tent had been erected near the riverbank. Most of the workers had left for the night, but a group of men were testing the lights that had been strung inside the tent. Emma and Cort stood at the entrance, watching, and Emma felt a pang of envy as she surveyed the scene. A wooden floor had been laid, and dozens of long tables with delicate white chairs ran the length of the tent, with a large space reserved for the musicians and a spacious dance floor. Long swathes of white netting had been draped from one side of the tent to the other, caught at the peak with lush bouquets of baby's breath. A profusion of twinkle lights and white paper globes hung suspended from the ceiling, and even the support posts had been wrapped in gauze and lights. The entire setting had an ethereal, otherworldly beauty.

Emma turned away, but a second, even larger dance floor had been built on the lawn itself, beneath a white pergola strung with a profusion of lights and bordered with flowers. Across the wide expanse of lawn, the ranch house sparkled and the sounds of music and laughter drifted toward them. There was literally no way to escape the wedding preparations.

She really shouldn't have come.

She'd thought she could get through the weekend with grace and dignity, but now she wasn't so sure. Her mother had been right; she'd likely only been extended an invitation out of duty, and not because anyone actually wanted her there.

"I think I'll go to bed," she said morosely. "Feel free to stay up and join the festivities. My brother Holt would probably love to talk to you about bull riding. Maybe even bull breeding. He's into that stuff."

Hands reached for her, turning her to face him. Light from the tent spilled over Cort's face, and Emma could see a glint of gentle amusement in his eyes. "I didn't take you for a coward, Emmaline Claiborne."

Somewhere close by, a dog began to bark with excitement.

"What am I even doing here?" she asked him, embarrassingly close to tears.

"Hey," he said softly, and pulled her into his arms. "You're a Claiborne, remember? You're here to show them that you're not beaten. Not by a long shot."

Emma tried to laugh, but the sound turned into a sort of sniffling sob. "Try telling that to my mother. She says I'm barely a Claiborne." She gave an agonized groan. "I should have stayed in New York."

But Cort only laughed and slid a hand to the nape of her neck, cradling her scalp. "What did you say the family motto is? *Do the right thing*? Darlin', I think you're doing exactly the right thing by being here this weekend."

Emma was transfixed by the way the light from the tent

played across his features, and how his eyes seemed to glow in his tanned face. Then her gaze dropped to his mouth, and she was lost. Hardly aware of doing so, she tipped her face up, inviting his kiss.

Then she jerked away from him as a shrill scream split the air.

Chapter Eight

ALREADY ALERTED BY the frantic barking of the dog, the high-pitched screech galvanized Cort into action. Before the scream had fully faded, he was turning away from Emma and heading toward the river at a run.

"Go get help!" he yelled over his shoulder.

He didn't wait to see if she obeyed, but sprinted toward the spot where the dog still barked incessantly. The underbrush grew heavy and dense by the water, and outside the circle of light from the wedding tent, the darkness was almost complete. Cort shoved his way through some low brambles, not even feeling the prickers that snagged his clothing and skin. He skidded to a halt as he reached the embankment of the river, and the ground fell away beneath his feet. He could hear a child crying, and a second child yelling something unintelligible and above that, the endless barking.

In the gloom, he could see a boy stretched out on his stomach on the ground, his upper body hanging over the embankment as he reached for something. Not something, Cort realized in horror, but *someone*. A child had fallen into the river, and now the embankment was too steep and too slippery with mud to climb back out. The dog ran in short bursts back and forth along the bank, barking his alarm.

"Here, let me," Cort called, and scrambled over to the boy, while another child stood nearby, crying. Two plastic jars lay forgotten in the tall grass, illuminated by the lightning bugs inside.

"I can't reach her!" the boy yelled.

Cort peered over the embankment and saw a little girl in the water, clinging to a half-submerged log that had washed up near the shore. She looked to be no more than five years old, and her pale little face was bleached with terror. Even as he quickly assessed the situation, her short arms slipped from the log, which was slick with water and slime. In an instant, she vanished beneath the dark surface of the river.

Shit.

"Stay back!" he instructed the children, and then plunged boots first into the murky waters of the Pedernales.

The water was up to his neck. Ducking beneath the surface, he fished blindly for the little girl, but his hands encountered emptiness. Even with his eyes open, there was only blackness. After endless minutes, he broke the surface and dragged in a lungful of air before pushing himself back beneath the water, this time moving downstream with the current and sweeping his arms in a wide arc.

Just when his lungs felt as if they would explode, his fingers brushed against something soft and pliant. He snatched at it, and realized he had the girl's bare foot in his hand. Pulling her toward him, he hooked an arm around her and broke the surface, sucking in air and pushing himself toward the nearest embankment, keeping the little girl's head above water. She was limp and unresponsive in his arms. The current had pushed them downstream to an area where the banking wasn't as steep as it had been where they had gone in. Slogging his way through the shallows, Cort carried the child to the grass and laid her down gently, wiping riverweed away from her face.

"C'mon, sweetheart," he muttered, and bent his head to her mouth, hoping to feel a breath, however faint. Water dripped from his hair onto her pale face. Unable to detect any breathing or a heartbeat, he tipped her head back, pinched her nose closed, and gave her two slow, gentle breaths. He'd taken a CPR class several years before, but he'd never had to use the training until now. Using the palm of his hand, he did five quick chest compressions, and then repeated the rescue breathing.

Cort heard voices in the distance, and glanced up just long enough to see a dozen or more flashlights bobbing toward him in the darkness. He didn't stop, but continued his lifesaving efforts, alternating between chest compressions and breathing, silently praying for the little girl to come around.

"Cort! Cort!"

He heard Emma shouting his name, and he paused just long enough to let them know where he was. "Over here!"

In the next instant, Holt and Emma were there, crashing through the underbrush, followed by Gus and Evan, Callie and Damon, and at least a dozen other guests from the main house. One of Callie's bridesmaids promptly began screaming when she saw the child Cort was desperately working to save.

"Oh my God, Lucy! She's my daughter! Please—" She tried to surge forward, but Holt restrained her.

"Let him do this," he said gravely.

The woman was sobbing now, and she turned her face into Holt's shoulder.

Emma crouched down across from Cort. "Do you want someone to take over?" she asked, her voice gentle. "Evan is here, and he's an experienced EMT. You must be getting tired."

Cort shook his head, but didn't say anything. He didn't want to lose count of the compressions. He knew it looked bad for the little girl, but he refused to give up. How long had it been since she'd gone into the water? Five minutes? Ten minutes? Longer? Time had stopped, and he no longer had any idea.

"Cort, maybe—"

He shot her a determined look. "*Don't.*"

In that instant, the little body beneath his hands spasmed, and they both started in surprise. Immediately, Cort turned the little girl onto her side and she vomited a stream of water, and then began to cough and cry weakly.

"Oh, thank God!" her mother cried. "*Lucy!*"

"Good girl," Cort said, keeping his voice reassuring and calm. He held the child as she continued to gag. "You're okay. You're going to be okay."

The little girl was crying loud and in earnest now, so Holt released her mother, who fell to her knees in the grass and clutched the child to her. For a moment, Cort could only kneel in the grass, hands braced on his thighs as he drew in deep, steadying breaths. The little girl *would* be okay.

Emma crouched beside him, and he raised his head to look at her.

"Cort," she murmured, and put a hand to his cheek. "Are you okay? What you just did—"

"I did what anyone would have done."

"No," she said softly, searching his eyes. "You saved her life."

"The other two kids? They're okay?"

Emma nodded. "They're shaken up a bit, but they're fine. They're up at the house now, waiting."

Cort nodded. "Glad they're okay."

"I can hear the ambulance arriving," Gus said. Leaning over, he spoke to the girl's mother. "Christine, why don't you let Holt carry Lucy up to the house? You can ride with her to the hospital."

Leaning down, Holt lifted the child in his arms, and Christine clutched her daughter's hand as they walked back across the lawn. Most of the others went with them, their flashlights cutting beams of light across the grass as they made their way toward the house, where an ambulance was pulling down the long driveway.

Evan extended a hand to Cort and helped him to his feet. "Thank God you were able to save her. Our family has known Christine since she was a kid. We went to Lucy's christening. If anything had happened to her—"

"I'm just glad she's okay," Cort said.

"We all are," Gus replied. "I've been friends with Lucy's grandfather for more than fifty years. I could never have looked him in the eye again if something had happened to Lucy while she was under my care."

There was a brief silence as they each contemplated what could have been.

"Well, you wouldn't have been so lucky if that had been the East River," Damon commented. He still held a bottle of beer in his hand, and now he pointed it toward the water. "This river looks pretty shallow and slow-moving, so you had that in your favor."

Cort stared at the other man in disbelief. Beside him, he felt Emma go rigid with outrage.

"Don't you dare make light of what Cort did," she said. Her voice trembled with emotion. "That river is deceptively calm-looking on the surface, but there's a strong current and it's deeper than you realize. The fact that Lucy was swept under in the dark and he *still* managed to find her is a miracle."

Damon stared at them both, and said something under his breath that sounded suspiciously like *Whatever* before he took a hefty swig of his beer.

"Emma's right," Evan said. "We've seen more than one adult drown in this river over the years."

"Cort," Gus said after a moment, "you look as if you could use a change of clothes and a stiff drink."

Until that moment, Cort hadn't been aware of how his clothing clung to him, heavy and wet with river water. "Yes, sir," he said. "I'll take the drink first, if you don't mind."

Gus chuckled and clapped him on the back. "Well done, son. We all owe you a debt of gratitude for what you did tonight."

As Gus and the other men turned away, Cort toed off one of his boots and upended it, allowing a stream of water to pour out. Emma waited as he did the same with the other boot.

"I hope they're not ruined," she said, eyeing the boots as he carried them in one hand and fell into step beside her.

"Nah, they'll be fine. I keep them well-oiled, so once they dry out, they'll be as good as new."

Seemingly on impulse, Emma wrapped both arms around his waist and hugged him tightly.

"Whoa," Cort said, holding his arm away from her. "You don't want to be doing that, honey. I'm dripping wet."

"I don't care," she said. "I'm just so glad you're both okay."

Cort could feel the heat from her body seeping through his wet clothes and warming him wherever they touched. Up ahead, Damon watched them over his shoulder, and Cort knew Emma's impulsive display of affection had been for the other man's benefit. With a self-deprecating laugh, Cort put his free arm around her shoulders and pulled her closer. He was an idiot. For just a moment, he'd really thought Emma had been relieved for his safety. But he'd known the deal when he'd agreed to come to Last Stand with her, so now he pressed his lips against her temple, feeling a surge of satisfaction when Damon frowned and turned his attention forward again. As they followed the other men back toward the house, something caught Cort's eye in the tall grass near the river.

"Hold on a second," he said. "Stay right here."

Emma released him, and stepping gingerly in his stocking feet, Cort made his way back toward the riverbank. There in the grass lay the two plastic bug jars, with their tiny inhabitants blinking inside. Scooping them up, he carried the jars back to where Emma waited for him.

"What should we do with these?" he asked. "Release the little guys?"

"Let's bring them up to the house, and then the kids can release them." Emma took both jars from him, cradling them in one arm as she reached for Cort's free hand. "Daddy will have a drink waiting for you, and then you can change your clothes."

By the time they reached the house, the ambulance was just pulling away, and the guests had mostly returned to the patio to talk about the evening's dramatic events. Only Gus, Holt, and Evan waited for them near the front entry.

"Why don't you go have that drink," Emma suggested, "and I'll return the bug jars to the kids."

Cort watched her go, suppressing a smile as he saw the left side of her shirt was wet with water from where she had pressed against him, and nearly transparent. Realizing the Claiborne men were waiting for him, he set his boots on the porch and followed them into the house.

"I should probably go change first," he demurred, as they entered Gus's office and he got a look at the expensive leather furnishings.

"Nonsense," Gus said, and moved to a sidebar where several bottles of good liquor stood on a tray next to a collection of snifters and rocks glasses. "What's your preference? Bourbon? Whiskey? Tequila?"

"Bourbon, please."

Gus poured two fingers of bourbon into four glasses, and handed one to each of them. Raising his glass, he looked at Cort. "To brave men with good reflexes. Glad you're here, Cort Channing."

They each raised their glasses, and Cort took a long swallow of the bourbon, welcoming the burn at the back of his throat, and the way it warmed him all the way down. The room was silent for several minutes, as they savored the bourbon. Beyond the closed door of the study, Cort could hear guests saying their good-byes. He guessed the party was over. He couldn't blame anyone for not wanting to celebrate in the wake of the near-tragedy, but was mildly surprised that neither Gus nor his sons seemed inclined to bid farewell to any of the guests. Even more interesting, Gus had not invited Damon to join them in their toast.

"Speaking of good reflexes," Holt said after a moment, "I finally figured out why you look familiar."

Cort groaned inwardly, knowing what was coming. He didn't respond to Holt's statement, but just gave the other man a questioning look.

"I watched you ride a A Bull Named Sue at the San Antonio Stock Show and Rodeo about four months ago," Holt said. "That bull was pure hell on hooves, and you rode him all the way to the buzzer."

"I did," Cort agreed.

"You're a bull rider, eh?" Gus asked, his blue eyes sharpening on Cort. "Are you pro?"

"Not yet, sir," Cort said. "I'm doing well in the semi-pro circuits, and I'm hoping to get to the Las Vegas invitational at the end of the year."

"How long have you been riding?" asked Evan.

"I sat my first bull when I was twelve, began riding for money in high school, and went semi-pro when I turned twenty-two."

"So you've been at this for what—five or six years?"

"I've been at it for more than fifteen years," Cort corrected him, "but I only got serious about it six years ago."

"That's a hard way to earn a paycheck," Gus commented.

"I do okay." No way was he going to talk money with the Claiborne family. Cort had saved every damned penny he could spare since he'd left his granddad's ranch years earlier, but even as much as he'd managed to put away, he knew it was nothing next to what the Claibornes had.

"You planning to ride bulls until you're too old, too worn out, or too broken to continue?" Gus asked.

"No, sir. I'm looking to buy some property and start my own ranch," he said smoothly.

Cort still wasn't ready to tell them he was Hank Walker's grandson. Folks around here had long memories, and eventually someone would put two and two together, and remember what had happened to his mother, Bobbi Walker Channing, all those years ago. Worse, they might remember his father, Roy Channing. The Claibornes would judge him for what his father had done, and he wouldn't blame them. But the real reason he was reluctant to talk about his granddad was because he didn't want Holt to start thinking about the Walker stud seed.

He'd heard rumblings that Holt Claiborne was looking to start his own breeding program for bucking bulls. Maybe he already knew that the Double U Ranch was going up for auction in just a few short months. He doubted Holt would be interested in purchasing land outside of Last Stand, but if he knew the ranch was being auctioned part and parcel along with Hank Walker's collection of champion bull seed, Holt would definitely be interested. He'd haul in his big lawyers and his big money, and bury any chance Cort had of keeping the property in the family.

He owed his mother—and his granddad—that much. He didn't think he'd ever be able to forgive Roy Channing for what he did to his mother and granddad, but maybe he could let go of some of the guilt he carried for being his son.

So instead of volunteering that information, he kept it to himself.

"There's plenty of good land here in Last Stand," Gus said, thoughtful. "You should take a look, maybe something will appeal to you."

The significance of the statement wasn't lost on Cort. By suggesting he settle in Last Stand, Gus Claiborne was all but giving his stamp of approval on Cort's relationship with Emmaline.

"I'll do that, sir," he lied.

"If you're interested," Holt said conversationally, "Evan and I are heading out in the morning to check on a herd on the south pasture. We saddle up at dawn, and should be back in time for breakfast." The glint in Holt's eyes as he extended the offer was almost challenging. But if he expected Cort to refuse, he was in for a disappointment. Cort had worked cattle from the time he was old enough to ride. He was as familiar with ranching as he was with bull riding, and he looked forward to being back in a saddle. Evan grinned, and the devilish expression in his blue eyes warned Cort that this was likely to be a test of some sort.

"That sounds like an offer I can't refuse. I'll plan on it." He finished his bourbon and set the glass down on the sidebar. "Thanks for the drink, but if you'll excuse me, I think I'll get into some dry clothes."

He left the private office with a sense of relief. He had been certain Emma's father would press him for the name of his granddad, and he wasn't sure he'd have been able to avoid telling him the truth. Anyone in the cattle business in this part of Texas knew who Hank Walker was.

The hallway was empty when he left the study, and he took the stairs to the upper level of the house two at a time, unbuttoning his soggy shirt as he went. By the time he reached Emma's bedroom, he was stripping the wet garment away from his body and rolling it into a sodden ball. He stepped into the dark bedroom and pulled the door closed before he unbuttoned his jeans and pushed them down to his ankles, stepping out of them and peeling his wet socks from his feet. He desperately needed a shower to rid himself of the smell of mud and river water.

As he crossed the room in his boxer briefs, the ensuite bathroom door opened and Emma emerged, wreathed in a swirling cloud of steam, her nearly naked body silhouetted against the bright light of the bathroom.

Cort went still, and for a moment he forgot to breathe.

She wore nothing but a towel wrapped around her body, and her bare shoulders and legs gleamed wetly from the shower she'd just taken. Her long hair had been pinned up at the top of her head, and loose tendrils curled damply around her shoulders. Cort had never seen anything so sexy, and his treacherous body reacted immediately.

"Cort," she exclaimed, and her hands went up to clutch the towel more securely. "I didn't—I wasn't—I thought you were with my father."

"I was." He saw surprise and trepidation on her face, but there was something else there too. Something that looked like anticipation. "I need a shower and clean clothes. I didn't know you'd be up here."

He took a step closer to her, and she flattened herself against the doorjamb, as if she expected him to push past her. But he didn't. He couldn't have moved past her if his life depended on it. Instead, he stopped with just six inches of space separating them, enough that he wasn't actually touching her, but close enough that he could feel the heat from her body, see the tiny pulse throbbing like crazy at the base of her smooth throat, and smell the clean, fragrant scent of her soap and shampoo. She was every fantasy he'd ever had, every birthday and Christmas wish he'd ever made.

He let his gaze drift over her, taking in her smooth brow and cheeks, the elegant sweep of black eyebrows, the way her long lashes spiked with moisture over her downcast eyes. Her lips, pink and lush, were parted and her breath came quickly. Lower, a flush of color began to creep upward from beneath the edge of the terrycloth, which had slipped just enough for him to glimpse the sweet valley between her breasts.

"Cort..." Her voice was husky.

Lifting his gaze, he found her attention riveted on his mouth with an expression so hot and needy, Cort felt it all the way to his toes. Beneath the damp fabric of his boxer briefs, he grew even harder. There was no way he could resist. It would be like a man in hell refusing a slaking drink of cool water. He knew kissing her was a bad idea, that she was vulnerable and hurting, and anything he had to offer her would only be a temporary distraction.

She didn't want him. But his body didn't care, and his pulse pounded hotly in his ears.

"Emmaline."

She lifted her eyes to his, and the shared heat almost incinerated him. He could stand there and spontaneously combust, or he could quench the flames. Bending his head, he covered her mouth with his own, and everything seemed to come together in a white-hot rush of pleasure. The shock of it was so intense that an involuntary sound escaped Cort's throat, a deep grunt that was a mix of satisfaction and frustration. That small noise seemed to enflame Emma, and she slanted her mouth to allow him better access. There was nothing tentative or shy about her response. She locked on to his mouth, feasting on his lips with an urgency that caused his balls to tighten, and his stomach muscles to contract with need.

Cort forced himself to go slow, when everything in him wanted to haul her against his aching body and ravage her. Instead, he braced one hand on the doorjamb above her head, careful not to touch her with any other part of his body. She was too confused about her feelings, and too vulnerable for him to take advantage of her that way. This desperate, moist fusing of their mouths had to be enough.

For now.

"Cort," she gasped, dragging her mouth free as one hand went to the nape of his neck. Her fingers were cool against his hot skin. "Take me to bed."

Her words stunned him, galvanized him. Bending his head, he deepened the kiss, sinking his tongue into her mouth and licking her. She tasted like minty toothpaste, but beneath that, he could taste *her*. He didn't realize she'd shifted closer until he felt the soft terrycloth of the towel against his naked chest and the rapid rise and fall of her breasts. But when she slid an arm around his neck and pressed closer, some small vestige of sanity returned.

Breaking the kiss, Cort pressed his forehead against hers, and their breath mingled in warm pants. He wanted her more than he'd ever wanted another woman, but not like this. Not when she was using him as a substitute for the man she really wanted, but couldn't have. He knew he could make it good for her, could have her writhing with pleasure beneath him, and the temptation to accept her offer was almost more than he could resist. But she was still too emotionally wrapped up in her ex. When he finally slept with Emmaline, she would have no illusions about who it was making love to her. With difficulty, he stepped back, putting distance between them. He brushed the backs of his fingers along her flushed cheek.

"Go to bed, honey. I'm not what you need right now."

"You're exactly what I need. Please, Cort…"

Her eyes, hazy with desire, pleaded with him, and Cort found his resistance slipping. It took all his restraint not to haul her back into his arms. "Not tonight, sweetheart. We both know you only asked me to sleep in your room so you could make Damon jealous, but that's not enough reason to jump into something you'll regret in the morning."

He wouldn't regret a damn thing, but she would, and that was enough to keep him from reaching for her again. Her gaze dropped to his rampant arousal, and Cort could almost see the thoughts racing through her mind. *Even her fake boyfriend didn't want her.* Cort could have dissuaded her from that belief, could have spent the entire night showing her just how much he did want her, in every way a man could want a woman. But she would hate him in the morning. And that sobering thought was all it took for him to not stop her when she made an inarticulate sound of frustration and fled, all but slamming the bathroom door in his face. Expelling a harsh breath, he dropped his head onto his arm, still braced against the door frame.

He was in serious trouble.

He'd thought he could spend the weekend with her and

let her use him in whatever way she needed. He'd even thought he could entice her into his bed, and then let her walk away when the weekend was over.

He'd been wrong.

Chapter Nine

BRINGING CORT CHANNING to the wedding had been a mistake. But the biggest mistake had been letting her attraction to him overrule her good sense. She'd wanted him so badly, wanted him still. She'd just about melted all over him. And yet he'd rejected her. Emma's face burned just thinking about it. There was absolutely no way she was going to be caught in that bed when he finally came out of the bathroom, especially when he'd made it clear he wasn't going to join her there. Instead, she dressed as quickly as she could in the dark bedroom, rifling through her suitcase until she found a cotton boho skirt with an elastic waistband, and a sleeveless blouse.

The sound of the shower was torture as she imagined Cort standing beneath the spray of water, naked and aroused. Had he given himself relief? Or did his body still ache the way hers did, with unslaked desire? Just the memory of that rigid rise of flesh beneath his cotton briefs brought a rush of heat to her skin, and the soft, wet place between her legs pulsed with unfulfilled need.

She was such an idiot.

Gathering her wet towel and discarded clothing, she

stepped on Cort's soggy jeans and shirt in the dark, and quickly scooped those up, as well. She needed to get away, to put as much distance as possible between herself and the hard, handsome hunk of man in the shower, before she did something *really* stupid. Like strip herself bare and join him. Not a smart idea, since he'd made it clear he wasn't going to go there with her. He'd implied she was only using him to make Damon jealous, but her ex-boyfriend had been the last thing on her mind when Cort had kissed her.

She made her way downstairs to the laundry room next to the kitchen, and as she dropped her and Cort's clothing into the washing machine, felt something bulky in his pockets. She withdrew his wallet and his phone, and set them aside before she checked his other pockets. After she programmed the wash cycle, she took his wallet and phone back upstairs. The leather was soaked through, and his phone was likely ruined. Outside the doorway to her bedroom, she paused and turned the wallet over in her hands. She would just look, to be sure nothing had been irreparably damaged. Pushing down the guilt, she opened the wallet, disappointed when she found only the usual IDs and credit cards. She was about to close it again, when she saw a small photo tucked behind his license. She pulled it out and studied it.

The picture was of Cort when he was a toddler, sitting on the lap of a pretty woman. The resemblance between the two was striking, and Emma knew the woman had to be his mother. They were looking at each other and laughing, and Emma felt her heart catch. The photographer had caught a beautiful moment. She slid the photo back into place quickly before Cort could finish his shower and catch her. She opened the bedroom door and laid the wallet and phone on the dresser, where he would see them. Then she quickly made her way back downstairs.

Cocking her head, she realized the music had stopped playing, and the house seemed unusually quiet. She found Rosa-Maria and Jessie in the kitchen, packing up the food that only an hour earlier had been meant for the buffet.

"What's going on?" she asked, and craned her neck to look through the French doors at the terrace. The fairy lights still glittered, but she heard no conversation, no laughter, no clink of glasses or dishware. "Did everybody leave?"

Jessie paused in the act of covering a container filled with spicy rice and beans. "After what happened, nobody felt much like celebrating. Callie and her bridesmaids have gone to the hospital to be with Christine. Once they left, pretty much everybody else decided to leave too."

"I'm so sorry. I hope the food won't be wasted."

"Of course not," Jessie assured her. "I'll leave enough here for the family and any guests who might come for lunch tomorrow, and I'll bring the rest over to the community center."

"Has there been any word on Lucy's condition?" Emma asked.

"Callie called and said they are keeping her overnight, but only as a precaution." Jessie looked up, and a smile lit her dark eyes. "Thanks to your boyfriend, she's going to make a full recovery."

"Oh, thank goodness."

"And how is Cort doing? That was a very brave thing he did."

"He's fine. I left him in the shower." Immediately, hot color rushed into her face at the implication in her words. "I mean, he needed a shower, and—"

Jessie watched Emma with a delighted glint in her eyes before she burst out laughing. "I don't know why you're embarrassed. He's a gorgeous man. In fact, I don't know why you're down here, when he's up there!" Her voice dropped to a conspiratorial whisper. "*Naked!*"

Emma didn't want to talk about Cort, or even think about him upstairs in the shower, and sought to change the subject. "What can I do to help you?"

"Would you mind bringing in the dishes from the terrace? I'll load up the dishwasher before I leave."

"Of course!" Grateful for something to do, Emma stepped out onto the terrace and began collecting champagne flutes, glassware, and beer bottles together onto one table. She realized the music hadn't been turned off as she'd earlier thought, but the volume had been turned down so low as to be barely discernable in the background.

The bartender was breaking down the bar and putting away the alcohol and mixers, and one of the girls who had earlier been passing hors d'oerves was now picking up trash and wiping down tables. Soon, even they left, and Emma found herself alone on the terrace with only the soft strains of music to keep her company.

As she loaded the glassware onto a tray, she looked

around at the empty patio and felt an unexpected pang of sympathy for Callie. The earlier festive atmosphere had vanished, and now the place had all the joy of a morning-after hangover.

A large ice bucket stood in one corner of the patio, and Emma saw a single, longneck bottle protruding from the melting ice. Retrieving it, she popped the cap and sank into a chair. After the events of the day, nothing had ever tasted as good as the cold beer, and she took a long swig, before closing her eyes and putting her head back. She just needed a few moments to gather her thoughts and put things back in perspective.

But as soon as she closed her eyes, images of Cort flood-ed her mind. Again, she saw his six-pack abs, the heavy muscles of his chest with its light furring, and the sculpted curves of his shoulders. She recalled once more the sensation of his mouth, the silken stroke of his tongue, and the sound he'd made deep in his throat when she'd responded to that molten kiss. That sound had caused her to liquefy in his arms.

"Emma."

The deep voice made her eyes pop open. Damon stood several feet away, hands shoved in his pockets as he watched her. He looked disheveled, as if he'd been pushing his fingers through his hair, and his shirt was rumpled and partly untucked. He swayed slightly. Emma pushed herself straighter in her chair, aware that her heart had begun to thump hard against her ribs. The last person she wanted to see right now was Damon Stewart. Her gaze flickered to the house, but there was no sign of either Rosa-Maria or Jessie.

"Damon. What are you doing here? I thought you'd be at the hospital with Callie."

He shrugged. "She has her girlfriends; I'd only be in the way."

Emma set her bottle of beer on the table and rose to her feet. No way did she want to be alone with Damon. They had nothing to say to one another that they wouldn't both regret later. She gestured toward the assortment of glassware and bottles on the nearby table. "Well, I should probably bring these dirty glasses into the kitchen, and then go to bed."

As she stepped past him, Damon caught her, his fingers manacling her wrist. "Wait. I've been hoping to get you alone." Seeing her expression, his eyes widened. "Just to talk, nothing else!"

Emma wanted to yank her arm free, but instead she gave him a tolerant look. "Why? What could we possibly have to talk about?"

"This past year has been difficult," he said, his expression earnest. Reaching down, he caught hold of both her hands, squeezing her fingers. "Do you know what it's like when your future in-laws treat you with perfect politeness, but you know that behind your back, they're talking about what an asshole they think you are?"

His words were slightly slurred, and Emma realized he'd had too much to drink. His palms were damp and she tried to pull her hands free. "I actually don't know what that's like and what's more, I don't really care," she said. "But while we're on the subject, let me remind you that I am about to become one of those perfectly polite in-laws, because you're marrying *my sister* in two days. Now let me go, Damon."

"You can help me," he continued as if she hadn't spoken. "Talk to your father and brothers. Tell them I love Callie. I really do, and I want them to know that. I'm not a bad guy, Ems, really."

Emma stared at him disbelief. "Are you serious? It's not enough that you dumped me for my own sister, now you expect me to put in a good word for you with my father and brothers?"

"I never meant to hurt you. I love Callie, but I see the way she looks at me sometimes, as if she has doubts." His fingers tightened almost painfully around hers. "You have every reason to hate me, and I know you don't care, now that you have your cowboy—" He broke off, and his face twisted almost comically as a new thought occurred to him. "How did you two meet, anyway?"

"Okay, that's enough," Emma said, exasperated. Oddly, her previous anger toward Damon had evaporated and now she felt only pity for him. "You've had too much to drink and you're going to feel like an idiot in the morning. Please let me go."

"I just can't lose her." To Emma's horror and astonishment, Damon looked as if he was about to cry. Without warning, he threw his arms around Emma, hugging her so tightly she could hardly breathe. "Please, Emma."

"Damon," she protested, her voice muffled against his shoulder. Her hands were wedged between their bodies, and she pushed against his chest in a futile effort to break free. She turned her face to demand he release her at the same instant he turned his head to speak, and their mouths collided. For a scant instant, Emma was too surprised to react, although she knew the brief contact was an accident.

"Damon!" Callie's shocked voice cut through the air.

Emma and Damon leapt apart, and from Callie's outraged expression, Emma knew they both looked guilty as hell. Worse, in the kitchen behind her stood Cort and Jessie. Cort's expression was shuttered, but Jessie's eyes were round with surprise. Behind Cort's back, Jessie gave her an astonished look and mouthed the words, *What was that?*

"This isn't what you think," Emma began, knowing full well if you had to say that, it probably wasn't true.

"Callie, sweetie, I was just telling Emma how much I love you," Damon said, starting toward her. "This was nothing, just a hug between friends."

Callie put her hands up as if to ward him off, her gaze flying between them. "You know what? It's been a long day and I just want to go to bed. I'll ask Holt to drive us to my mother's house."

She turned and pushed past Cort and Jessie as Damon hurried to follow her, declaring both his innocence and his love for her.

"That really wasn't what you think!" Emma said, looking directly at Cort. "I had no idea he was going to grab me like that!"

Jessie glanced between the two of them, clearly wishing she was anywhere else in the world at that moment. "Well.

I'm just about finished here, so I'm going to bring these bins out to the truck and then I'm off. Good night."

"I'll give you a hand," Cort offered, and with one last look at Emma, turned and walked away.

Emma lowered herself into a nearby chair. Bending forward, she covered her face with her hands. She knew how the scene had looked, but she also knew the more she protested her innocence, the guiltier she appeared.

She shouldn't have come. She realized that now. She'd only made things worse, both for Callie and for herself. She could still see Colt's face when she'd pulled free of Damon's embrace. If she didn't know better, she'd have thought he looked disappointed, but maybe that had been her imagination. And anyway, he'd known the deal when he'd agreed to come with her to Last Stand. There was no reason for her to feel as if she'd been caught cheating, especially when he'd been the one who'd pushed her away earlier.

"What's wrong, darlin'? You look as if someone just kicked your dog."

Emma raised her head to see her father standing in front of her. "Oh, Daddy," she sighed, and stood up, moving into his embrace. "I'm such an idiot."

"Does your idiocy have anything to do with why Callie and Damon just hightailed it out of here, or why your young man looks to be in a horns-and-rattles mood?"

Emma gave a choked laugh. "I swear I did *nothing*."

Her father released her and amusement sparkled in his blue eyes. "If I had a nickel for every time I've heard you say that, I'd be a wealthy man."

"I'm pretty sure you *are* a wealthy man," she said with a wry smile, and then dragged in a deep breath. "Damon thinks you all dislike him. He apologized for hurting me, said he loved Callie, and asked me to put in a good word for him with you and Holt. And then he hugged me."

"That doesn't sound so terrible."

"Callie and Cort only saw the hugging part," she said morosely, not mentioning the near-kiss, "but I swear I did nothing to encourage it."

"Hmm. Maybe I understand why Cort looked so put out. You never want to see your girl in another man's arms, especially when that other man is an ex. But he seems like a reasonable man, so I'm sure he'll understand."

She wasn't Cort's girl, but she couldn't tell her father that, either. This whole charade was for the sole purpose of convincing her family and Damon that she wasn't heartbroken, that she had moved on and was happy. "He thinks I'm still in love with Damon."

"Are you?"

Emma looked at her father in surprise. "After everything that's happened? No." And then more emphatically, "No! Of course I'm not."

"I shouldn't worry too much, then. This will all blow over by tomorrow. As for Damon, I don't dislike *him*. I dislike what he did to you." He cupped her face in his hands. "You are my daughter and I don't want to see you unhappy."

Emma nodded. "I know. But Callie is your daughter, too, and apparently Damon is what makes her happy."

"Callie is too headstrong for her own good. She's competitive about everything, especially with you."

As disturbing as it was to hear her father confirm what she had always believed, Emma was grateful to know it hadn't been her imagination. Callie had always been competitive, even as a child. Emma acknowledged that while she loved her sister, she didn't always like her.

"It makes no sense," Emma protested. "I'm hardly ever here, so what is there to compete for?"

But Gus only chuckled and pressed a kiss against her forehead. "Get a good night's sleep. Everything will look brighter tomorrow, I promise."

"Okay." She started to turn away, and then paused. "Thank you, Daddy. I've missed you."

"I've missed you, too, Emmaline. It's nice to have you home."

Home.

With a start, Emma realized that Riverrun did feel like home, more than her loft ever had, more than her mother's elegant apartment on the Upper East Side, and even more than her grandparents' gracious country house, with its views of the Hudson River. Because as beautiful and stylish as those New York residences were, they were just buildings. Here, she had her brothers and her father and—as much as she was loath to admit it—her sister.

She had just reached the staircase when the front door opened, and Cort came in from outside. In the semidarkness of the foyer, he surveyed her without emotion.

"Cort…"

"It's okay, honey," he said, and his voice was gentle. "I'm

not judging you."

"There's nothing to judge," she exclaimed, irritated. "He was drunk. It was just a sloppy hug, and nothing more. It didn't mean anything."

"You sure about that?

"*Yes.*" Emma pressed her fingers to a spot between her eyebrows, where an insistent pain had begun to throb. "I'm not the one who steals boyfriends. Or fiancés. I leave that to my sister."

He watched her with an intensity that unsettled her. Although he was leaning casually against the newel post of the bottom stair, his hands deep in his pockets, she was acutely aware of him. He was all hard muscle and easy masculinity, and his green eyes glowed like the Texas sky before a summer storm.

"So what now?"

Emma stared at him. She knew he referred to what had happened—or hadn't happened—between them upstairs. Deliberately misunderstanding him, she tipped her chin up. "I'm going to bed now."

"Okay." He paused. "I'll be up later."

Emma couldn't prevent her indrawn breath. "You still intend to sleep in my room?"

"That was your idea, honey, not mine. But if it makes you feel easier, I'll be on the floor, so you won't even know I'm there. I'm riding out to the south pasture at dawn with your brothers, so I'll be gone when you wake up."

Emma started. "You're riding out with my brothers?"

"Yes, ma'am."

"It's probably a test of some kind," she informed him. "My brothers have a history of hazing my boyfriends."

Straightening, Cort gave her a lazy smile. "How many boyfriends have you brought home, Emmaline?"

Two, if you counted Cort, although technically, he wasn't really her boyfriend. As a teenager, Emma hadn't spent enough time in Last Stand to get herself a boyfriend, and then she'd turned eighteen and had pretty much stopped coming to the ranch altogether. But her brothers had hazed Damon the first time she'd brought him home, soliciting his help in castrating and branding the new calves. That had gone well enough, but when they'd tossed the bits and pieces onto a hot barrel lid and expected Damon to eat them, he'd lost his lunch all over his borrowed work boots. That had been years ago, but Holt, Evan, and Luke still laughed about it.

"They'll have something planned," she cautioned, ignoring his question. Her brothers weren't malicious, and they would never do anything dangerous, but she wouldn't put it past them to try to humiliate Cort, or at least see what he was made of.

"I can take care of myself," he assured her.

Emma climbed the stairs to her bedroom, aware of Cort's eyes on her the whole way. She had no doubts he could take care of himself. But she couldn't help wishing he would follow her upstairs, and take care of her too.

Chapter Ten

WHEN EMMA WOKE up the following morning, the only evidence that Cort had actually stayed in the room was a pillow and a neatly folded blanket on the chair next to the door. She'd lain awake in tense anticipation for what had seemed like hours, waiting for him to come up. She'd arranged a place for him on the floor with some extra blankets and pillows, and had left the bathroom light on with the door cracked. Her nerves had been raw just thinking about him sleeping in such close quarters, and she was certain she wouldn't sleep a wink, knowing he was within arm's reach. But she must have been more exhausted than she realized, because she hadn't heard him come upstairs, or leave again at dawn.

She showered quickly, and then stood in front of her closet and looked at the outfits she'd brought with her from New York. Already, the day promised to be warm and humid, and none of the dresses or tight jeans she'd packed appealed to her.

On impulse, she opened her dresser and saw her old clothes neatly folded inside. These were what she'd always referred to as her "ranch clothes." Comfortable cotton pants and shorts, T-shirts, and button-downs. On impulse, she pulled on a pair of brown cotton shorts and a white T-shirt with a deeply scooped neck and cap sleeves. She brushed her hair into a ponytail and slipped her feet into a pair of flat sandals. Except for a sweep of mascara and some lip gloss, she left her face devoid of makeup. Surveying herself in the mirror, she thought her mother would hardly recognize her. When she finally made her way downstairs, the house was already buzzing with activity.

"There you are." Rosa-Maria beamed when Emma entered the kitchen. "Breakfast is on the terrace this morning, and your papa is already out there."

"Are the guys back yet?" she asked, trying to sound casual.

"Not yet."

Emma poured herself a cup of coffee and carried it out to the terrace. The morning air was warm, and a soft breeze carried the scent of wildflowers and freshly mown grass. Emma paused for a moment and breathed deeply. The breakfast table had been set for five, but only her father was there, reading a newspaper.

"Good morning, Daddy," she said, and dropped a kiss onto his cheek.

Gus folded his newspaper and set it to one side. "Good morning, darlin'. How did you sleep?"

"Like a baby," she admitted. "I never heard Cort leave this morning." She looked out across the property toward the wedding tent, where several container trucks were parked. The sweeping lawn was covered with workmen, as the final preparations for the wedding ceremony were made. Beyond the tent, she could see the barns and outbuildings, but there was no sign of Cort or her brothers. "Shouldn't they be back by now?"

Gus chuckled. "Don't fret. They'll be by shortly." He looked up and smiled as Rosa-Maria carried a tray out to the terrace and began setting dishes on the table. Scrambled eggs, a platter of sausage and bacon, another with perfectly sliced steak, grilled potatoes, a bowl of fruit salad, a pitcher of orange juice, and a pot of coffee. "Thank you, Rosa. This all looks delicious. You spoil me."

To Emma's amazement, Rosa-Maria blushed like a schoolgirl. "Someone needs to, señor. You work too hard."

Gus gave a grunt of assent, and began scooping eggs and steak onto his plate. "What are your plans for the day, Emmaline?"

"I have to go into town this morning. I airmailed a wedding gift to the post office, since it was too big to bring on the plane," she said. "I didn't want it to be delivered here, in case Callie saw it. I'll need to wrap it."

"A painting?"

"How did you know?"

Gus chuckled. "Darlin', when have you not had a paintbrush in your hand?"

"Well, it seems lately I do more gallery shows of other people's work than I do painting my own pieces," she admitted. "I have a pretty good inventory, but Mom isn't sure my work resonates with her clients."

"I've always said city folk don't have a lick of sense," he

replied. Smiling, he covered her hand with his own and squeezed her fingers. "If they did, they wouldn't live in the city."

Emma thought of the painting, one of a series that featured oversized, abstract poppy blooms that seemed to explode off the canvas. The piece she'd selected for Callie had been done in hues of deep blues and greens, and Callie had admired it when she'd stayed with Emma that last summer. Back when Emma hadn't realized her sister and Damon were carrying on an affair literally beneath her nose.

"Ah, here come the boys now," Gus murmured.

Emma followed his gaze to where her brothers and Cort were walking across the grass from the direction of the barns. Cort had a pair of heavily tooled, leather chaps slung over one shoulder. They were laughing about something, and for a moment, Emma sat back and admired the sight. If the city girls could only see these three men with their Stetsons, their broad shoulders, and their long, easy strides, there would be a stampede toward Texas.

"Hey, honey," Cort said as he climbed the stone steps to the terrace. He bent and pressed a kiss to her cheek, and Emma caught the scent of leather and spicy soap that she had come to associate with him. "Sleep well?"

The kiss hadn't been real, had only been a part of the charade they'd been acting out since they'd arrived at Riverrun, but Emma still felt a surge of pleasure. She murmured something about having slept soundly, and watched beneath her eyelashes as Cort set his chaps down, and took the chair across from her. He looked good, all chiseled cheekbones, dark gold hair, and lean muscles.

"Did you have a good ride?" she asked.

Holt and Evan exchanged glances, and Emma didn't miss the humor that glinted in their blue eyes.

"It was a good morning," Cort said as he heaped eggs and steak onto his plate. "Been a while since I've ridden, but it felt good to be back in the saddle."

Evan chuckled. "Were you actually in the saddle? I couldn't tell with all the bouncing around going on."

"Oh, no," Emma breathed. "What did you do?"

"I'm guessing they had you ride Alixir," Gus said, sitting back and pinioning Cort with a sharp look. "How did you do?"

"There's a reason he's a bull rider," Evan said, and Emma didn't miss the admiration in his voice. "The guy has unbelievable reflexes. He managed to stay on Alixir."

"Wait," Emma said, interrupting them. "What is so special about Alixir?"

"He wasn't fully broke." Cort grinned. "Until today."

Emma put her fork down and stared at her brothers. "You put *a guest* on an unbroken horse?"

Evan shrugged. "He did fine. Saved us about another week's work in the paddock too." He gave Emma an unrepentant grin. "So it all worked out."

Emma had watched her brothers break young horses to a saddle before, and knew the process took time, patience, and trust. She couldn't believe they had put Cort on a horse that wasn't yet accustomed to having a rider.

"Honey, they're exaggerating," Cort said, reading her

expression. "Alixir was ready to be ridden, he just didn't know it. He's a fine animal, and neither of us are worse for the experience."

Emma wasn't mollified. She glared at Holt. "Someone could have been hurt."

"Nobody was hurt, Emmaline." Holt glanced at Cort. "He's an experienced rider, and he knows his way around cattle too."

"Thanks," Cort said, his tone wry.

"Which ranch in Banderas did you grow up on, Cort?" Gus asked. "I know most of the ranch owners in the Hill Country, but I can't place anyone named Channing."

"That's because I was raised by my grandfather," Cort said. "You may have heard of him. Hank Walker."

There was a moment of stunned silence.

"Hank Walker is your grandfather?" Holt asked.

"He was, yes."

Emma speared a chunk of cantaloupe and glanced at her brother. He looked slightly dazed by the news.

"I met your grandfather once," Gus said, his eyes thoughtful. "It was years ago, at one of the annual cattlemen conventions, maybe before you were even born. He'd already made a name for himself in the bull breeding industry. An interesting, complex man, as I recall."

"That's one way to describe him," Cort said, his mouth lifting in a wry smile. "Others might call him antisocial and ornery."

"Hank Walker raised some of the finest bulls the bull riding community has ever seen," Holt said. "One of his bulls sold for over half a million dollars. Hell, I remember a single straw of stud seed from Terminator sold for over twenty-five grand."

"That was a long time ago," Cort said, setting his fork down. "When my granddad died, he'd been out of the bull breeding business for many years."

"Didn't someone steal his best stud seed?" Holt persisted. "Six canisters of liquid nitrogen, containing the semen from some of the most prized bulls in the industry were stolen from his breeding barn. That must have been at least twenty years ago, and the police never did find out who took it." He shook his head. "A damned shame. That seed must have been worth a fortune."

"It was three canisters, and they were stolen twenty-five years ago," Cort said quietly. "The loss of that seed destroyed my granddad. He never recovered. In fact, he was so deep in debt when he passed that the bank took over the property."

"I did hear something about that," Holt mused. "The Double U Ranch, right? Isn't it going up for auction?"

"I'm going to buy it back," Cort said easily. "I have some money saved up, and if I can make it to Las Vegas, I think I'll have a good shot at winning the prize jackpot." He picked up his fork and gave Holt a look that bordered on challenging. "Should be enough. Not many people want to buy a run-down ranch."

"No," Holt agreed, holding Cort's eyes. "Not unless that run-down ranch happens to come with what was left of Hank Walker's collection of prize stud seed. Not all of the canisters were stolen during the theft. Granted, what's left isn't as fine as what was taken, but it's still prime."

For a moment, there was only silence. Cort shoveled a forkful of home fries into his mouth and chewed, but didn't say anything. The air between the two men vibrated with tension.

"You know," Holt continued conversationally, "I've been thinking about getting into the bucking bull business. There's good money in it, I hear. But to have stud seed from Hank Walker's bulls, well that would be something. Breeders would come from all over just to purchase that stock."

"Holt—" Emma protested. She had no idea if her brother was deliberately baiting Cort, or if there was some other reason for his sudden interest in Cort's business.

"It's okay, Emmaline," Cort said, his voice gentle. He wiped his mouth with his napkin and pushed his chair back. "Every man's got the right to pursue his own path. Thank you for breakfast. If you don't mind, I'm going to shower and change."

Emma watched until Cort left the terrace before she turned on her brother, anger simmering in her voice. "What was that all about?"

Holt rounded his eyes and gave her a look of surprised innocence. "What?"

Emma's mouth flattened. "Don't give me that, Holt Blaisdell Claiborne. You're up to something."

"What am I up to?"

Emma stood. "I don't know, but whatever it is, I don't like it." She leaned over the table until her face was scant inches away from his. "Be nice to Cort. I *like* him."

She realized it was no less than the truth. She liked him *a lot*. He'd done her a huge favor by agreeing to come to Riverrun with her for the weekend, and he didn't deserve to be needled by her family.

Holt held up both hands in surrender. "Okay, okay. Don't worry. Your boyfriend is safe with me."

Emma gave him one last look before dropping a kiss on her father's head. "I'm going into town."

"The rehearsal ceremony begins at six o'clock here on the lawn," Gus said, "and then we're heading over to the Dragonfly for dinner at eight o'clock."

"If you don't mind, I think I'll skip the rehearsal ceremony," Emma said. "Watching them walk down the aisle once will be enough for me."

"Bring Cort. Show him around town," Gus suggested. "If he hasn't been to Last Stand before, he might find the history interesting. And take him into the Western store."

Emma paused. "Why?"

"His boots are still wet," Holt said. "I don't think he was all that happy to ride out this morning wearing a pair of Luke's old sneakers."

Knowing Cort was in the shower, Emma didn't go up to the bedroom. No way was she going to catch him in his altogether. The memories of their last encounter in the bathroom were still etched onto her brain. Instead, she waited for him on the front porch, idly pushing a rocker with her foot as she watched the wedding preparations continue.

When finally she heard his footsteps on the staircase, she

stood up and watched him through the screen door. He'd changed into a short-sleeve button-down shirt with pockets on the front that hugged the muscles of his chest. He'd rolled the short sleeves up and Emma couldn't help but admire the smooth, strong bulge of his biceps, and the way the shirt emphasized his broad shoulders. He carried his hat in one hand, and for the first time, Emma noticed he wore sneakers.

"Hi," she said when he stopped on the other side of the screen door. "I have to go into town to pick something up at the post office. Do you mind driving me?"

Through the screen, he swept her with a quick, thorough glance. "Has anyone ever told you that you have great legs?"

"Thanks," she said, knowing she shouldn't feel so pleased by the casual observation. "I do lots of spin classes. I'm sorry about your boots."

Cort pushed through the door and bent down to pick up his boots from where he had left them on the porch the previous night. "I only brought the one pair, and they're still too wet to wear."

The tooled leather was dark with moisture. A cowboy wore his boots everywhere, no matter the occasion, so Emma could only guess how annoyed he must feel not to be able to wear them.

"There's a Western gear shop in town," she said. "We can stop in. Maybe they'll have something you'll like."

Using one hand, Cort settled his hat onto his head and Emma followed him to the truck, admiring his backside. Even in sneakers, the guy was seriously hot.

The drive into town took less than ten minutes, and although the day already promised to be blisteringly hot, Emma refused to let him turn the air-conditioning on in the truck.

"Do you remember the night we met?" she asked. "That was only three weeks ago, but it was cold and rainy in New York." She draped an arm out of the open window, letting the warm wind buffet her fingers. "I love this weather. The heat has never bothered me."

Cort chuckled, but left the windows open. Main Street was busy, even on a Friday morning, but Cort found a parking spot in front of Kolaches, the German bakery. Through the large glass windows, Emma could see the restaurant was nearly full. On the covered sidewalk in front of the restaurant, a family sat on a bench surveying a tourist map of the town. Next door, the owner of Yippee Ki Yay, the Western store, was just unlocking the door. They watched as she flipped the Closed sign over so that it read Open.

"I used to love coming to Kolaches for breakfast as a kid," Emma mused, studying the windows. "They make these authentic potato pancakes that are to die for. Of course, we didn't do it very often. My brothers have an amazing capacity for food, so going out for breakfast was never cheap."

"I think my granddad and I came through here once when I was a kid," Cort said. "I remember wanting to stop, but he just kept on driving."

Cort was peering through the windshield at the Western

store, studying the window display with its abundance of boots, hats, and gloves. Emma wondered what his childhood had been like. Looking at him now, she felt as if her heart might break for the boy he had once been, with no parents and a grandfather who apparently had not wanted him.

"Let's go in, shall we?" she prompted.

The interior of the shop was cool and dark, with wood flooring and limestone walls. Steel fans rotated lazily overhead, and country music played softly through hidden speakers. Behind the counter, a woman looked up and smiled in acknowledgment.

"You folks need any help, just let me know," she said.

"Smell that," Emma enthused, breathing deeply. "Is there anything that smells better than real leather?"

Cort stood beside her, and now he inclined his head fractionally and closed his eyes, breathing her in. "You," he finally said, opening his eyes and pinning her with his gaze. "You smell better than anything I've ever known."

Emma found herself transfixed by the expression in his sea-green eyes, and for a moment, it seemed even the overhead fans stopped whirring. With difficulty, Emma gathered herself and looked away from Cort, forcing herself back to her surroundings. There were racks of leather coats in every style and color, some with fringe and some without. Floor-to-ceiling shelves of stacked Western hats dominated one wall, and through a wide door that led to a back room, Emma could see rack after rack of Western boots.

"This way," she urged him, and took his hand.

Cort followed her through to the back room, and they

spent several minutes wandering up and down the aisles, looking at the array of boots.

"How do you choose?" Emma asked, selecting a pair of red, white, and blue boots in a flag motif.

"Here," Cort said, and pulled a pair of women's boots from a shelf. "Try these."

Emma sat down on a bench and kicked her sandals off. The boots had a tan-colored, distressed upper, and a black boot shaft with intricate stitching. Holding the first boot by the pull straps, she wiggled her foot inside.

"That feels pretty good," she said, smiling up at Cort. "But we're not here to buy boots for me, we're here to get boots for you."

"Try the other one."

Obediently, Emma pulled the second boot on, and stood up. The heel was higher than her sandals, and paired with her shorts and T-shirt, she knew she must look ridiculous.

"I can't wear these," she protested.

"Honey, take a look," Cort murmured, and turned her toward the full-length mirror behind her.

Emma surveyed her reflection with some surprise. The boots had a low rise, with room to spare around her calves. Her legs looked slim and toned, and Emma had to admit she looked…hot. Raising her eyes, she met Cort's gaze in the mirror. "I feel as if I should be dancing on a bar top to some honky-tonk country music."

"It's a good look on you."

"They're comfortable. Surprisingly comfortable."

Cort chuckled. "They suit you."

"Okay, I'll get them. I don't think I've owned a pair of cowboy boots since I was a little girl." Turning away from the mirror, she surveyed the racks of boots. "Now let's find something for you."

But Cort was already pulling a pair of boots down. "These will work."

They were a pair of brown Lucchese boots in a distressed leather that looked as if they'd already been worn by some hard-working cowboy and slipped back onto the store shelves.

"Really?" Emma asked. "You wouldn't rather have these?"

Cort eyed the shiny black boots she'd pulled down and shook his head. "No thanks. These will do just fine."

Toeing off the sneakers, he pulled the boots on, and Emma had to admit they did do just fine. Pulling his pant legs down over the boots, he stood up and walked around the room several times, testing the fit. Several women had come into the store, and now they watched Cort with unabashed delight. They were older than Emma, and would have fit right in on Fifth Avenue. With his Stetson and Wranglers, and his hard-muscled physique, Emma thought again that Cort was the real deal. The women apparently thought so too.

"Excuse me," the first woman said, her expression hopeful. "Would you mind posing for a picture with me? My girlfriends back home will never believe I met a real cowboy."

Cort was gracious and accommodating, posing with each

of the women as they giggled and preened for the camera. When they finally left, Cort gave Emma an embarrassed smile and shrugged. "Happens all the time, but usually when I'm in the arena. They're obviously not from Texas, or a man in cowboy boots wouldn't be enough to turn their heads."

Emma didn't want to tell him that he could turn any woman's head, regardless of what he was wearing. He really had no idea how attractive he was, and that just made him even more appealing.

"Well, if you're all set, we should pay up," she said.

"There's just one more thing," Cort said, and made his way into the main store, and the endless display of cowboy hats. After studying them for a long moment, he selected one made of woven straw, with a rawhide cord around the brim. Emma stood obediently while he placed the hat on her head and adjusted it to his liking. "There," he finally said. "Perfect."

Emma turned to look in the mirror, and suppressed a bubble of laughter.

"What is it?" Cort frowned. "You don't like it?"

"No," she assured him with a grin. "I love it! I'm just thinking of how my mother would react if she could see me now. All my life, she's told me I belong in New York and not Texas. That I'm a Germaine, and not a Claiborne. Half of those ridiculous clothes I brought were her choices, not mine. She would have a fit if she could see me now."

"If she could see you now," Cort said, dipping his head to look directly into her eyes, "she'd see a strong, beautiful woman who wears her Texas heritage as easily as she does her

New York pedigree. You don't have to choose, Emmaline. You can be both."

Emma flushed, moved by both his words and by the understanding in his eyes. "Careful," she murmured, "you're going to turn my head, now."

"I should be so lucky," he said gruffly. "C'mon, let's pay up and go find something cold to drink."

They brought the boots and hat to the counter, and the owner looked up with a smile. She was an attractive older woman with short wispy hair that accentuated her delicate bone structure. "All set? Oh, you chose one of my favorite pairs of boots," she said to Emma. "You are going to love these. They break in beautifully, and become more comfortable with age."

Emma glanced at Cort and smiled. "You have good taste."

"How would you like to pay?" the owner asked.

Cort withdrew his wallet and slid a credit card across the counter. "Put it all on this."

"Cort, no!" Emma protested. "I can't let you buy my boots and hat. Seriously, I have my own money and these cost a fortune!"

"It's nonnegotiable," he said easily, "especially since I picked them out for you. I didn't even give you a choice."

The owner picked up the card and read the name embossed on the front. "You're Cort Channing?"

"I am."

She smiled. "I'm Lilly Corbyn, and I'm sorry to tell you, but your money's no good here. The boots and the hat are on the house."

Cort went still. "What are you talking about? I can pay for them. I *want* to pay for them."

"After what you did last night for Christine Becker's little girl? I heard the whole story, including how you jumped into that river with your boots on. Please, it's the least I can do." She turned to Emma. "And you must be Gus Claiborne's daughter, Emmaline. I haven't seen you since you were small. I hardly recognized you. If it helps, I'll settle up with Gus for your boots and hat, but *your* boots"—she looked at Cort—"are most definitely on the house. Christine is a good friend of my own daughters, and losing little Lucy would have been—" She shuddered. "I can't even go there."

Cort frowned, clearly uncomfortable.

"Please, Mr. Channing," Lilly said quietly. "It really is the least this town can do, especially considering how your boots were ruined."

"They're not ruined," he said darkly. "They're just...wet."

"Thank you," Emma said firmly, and took the shopping bags from her. "I'll have my father settle up with you for my things."

Lilly shrugged. "I'll send him an invoice. Thank you for what you did, Cort."

They left the store, and Emma could see Cort felt uneasy with the transaction.

"Cort, you saved that little girl's life," she said. "If someone wants to do something nice for you in return, you should let them."

"It would be *nice* to buy me a beer, or a cup of coffee," he said, "but not a pair of boots that cost a week's wages."

"You are seriously underestimating the enormity of what you did."

"I did what anyone else in that situation would have done," he grumbled. "I don't need anything in return."

"But if it makes people feel better to show their appreciation, then you should just be gracious and accept it," she said matter-of-factly. Catching his arm, she pulled him over to the now vacant bench in front of the German bakery. "C'mon, I want to wear my week's worth of wages."

"You don't even have socks on," he said with a reluctant laugh.

"I don't care. I love these boots."

They put his sneakers and her sandals into the shopping bag, and Emma clapped her new hat onto her head. Standing up, she tested her boots by strutting experimentally up and down the boardwalk. "How do I look?"

"Keep it up, and you're going to cause a traffic accident," Cort said as a passing pickup truck gave an appreciative honk. Emma gave the driver a jaunty wave, and a grin lifted the corners of Cort's mouth. "I've created a monster."

"A monster who's hungry," she declared, and grabbed his hand, pulling him to his feet. "Let's go in and have some potato pancakes. You are going to love them."

"I'm sure I will," he said with a chuckle. "Among my many attributes, I'm also ridiculously easy to please."

As he held the door open for her, Emma slipped past him, thinking of a hundred different ways she'd like to test that statement.

Chapter Eleven

THE GERMAN BAKERY, Kolaches, was still doing a brisk business, but they found a table in the corner, and Cort enjoyed watching Emma's face as she looked happily around the restaurant. He couldn't understand why she'd stayed away from Last Stand for so long when, clearly, she loved the town and everything it represented.

Two women sat at the table closest to them, one very elderly and the other very young. They were enjoying a pot of tea and a plate of pastries. The older woman caught Cort's attention as she laughed at something her companion said. Despite her advanced years, her laugh was as bright and joyful as a girl's. She was a tiny, wiry woman with long gray hair that she wore in a braid, wrapped neatly around her head. Cort thought she looked like a throwback to when Last Stand had been a frontier town.

Noticing his curiosity, Emma leaned across the table and lowered her voice to a whisper. "That's Minna Herdmann. She's a legend in this town. Can you believe she's over a hundred years old? Every year, the town throws a huge birthday party in her honor."

As if she knew they were talking about her, Minna

turned her bright gaze on Cort, and smiled. Cort smiled back and touched the brim of his hat. "Morning, ma'am."

When he looked back at Emma, she rounded her eyes and slid a little lower in her chair, embarrassed at having been caught. Cort laughed, since she hadn't said anything bad about Minna, unless revealing someone's age was taboo. But Cort figured if you lived to be a centurion, you ought to be proud of it. He watched as Emma set her wrist wallet and her phone on the table beside her place setting. No sooner had she done so than her phone began to vibrate. She picked it up and glanced at it, before turning it facedown again.

"Everything okay?" he asked.

"Mm-hm." She nodded, but didn't offer an explanation.

They ordered their food, and as Cort sipped his coffee, her phone vibrated several more times. Each time she would glance at it, but wouldn't respond. Finally, with a grimace, she picked the phone up and turned off the notifications.

"What is it?" he asked with a grin.

She rolled her eyes. "That ridiculous dating app keeps sending me notifications."

"Notifications of what?" he asked, but he already knew.

"Guys I might be compatible with, but it's just silly. I don't even use the app anymore."

Something twisted low in Cort's gut at the thought of other guys—strangers—trying to hook up with Emma. "Why don't you just shut down your account?"

To his surprise, Emma glanced at him from under her lashes, and she lifted one shoulder in a shrug. "I don't know...maybe after we go back to our respective lives, I'll want to check them out."

"Is that what you want? To meet guys based on some machine-powered AI algorithm?" He couldn't keep the disapproval from his voice.

"I've heard of people who have found their soul mates through dating apps."

"You do realize that most dating apps don't actually want you to find your happily ever after, right?"

Emma frowned. "Why wouldn't they want that?"

"Because they only make money as long as you keep your account open and continue to pay the monthly fees. If you were to actually meet someone and close your account, they'd stop making money."

"Well, I wasn't having much success with online dating, anyway," she grumbled. "First dates are exhausting, and they rarely lead to second dates. Besides, I'm not really in the market for a long-term relationship. I only needed someone to come to the wedding with me, and I found you." She gave him a bright smile. "So it all worked out in the end, right?"

"Sure," Cort said. What else could he say? He found his good mood rapidly evaporating. He wanted Emmaline, but the timing was all wrong. She said she wasn't looking for a long-term relationship, but he knew instinctively she wasn't the kind of woman who did casual. Worse, she was the kind of woman who made a man want to put down roots, but Cort had nothing to offer her. Not yet, anyway.

She changed the subject, regaling him with stories from her childhood. Her face was expressive, her smile quick, and her laugh contagious. He noticed more than one head turn to admire her, and realized he felt content to just sit and watch her. He liked listening to her laugh. He wanted to bask in the sound. For the first time in a long time, the restless sense that he needed to be somewhere else, or needed to get back on the road, was gone. He was suddenly glad he'd been able to secure a slot at the upcoming rodeo, which meant he could remain in Last Stand for another two weeks.

"Were you and your sister close when you were kids?" he asked, but he thought he already knew the answer.

Emma shook her head. "Not really. She had her own group of friends here in Last Stand. Besides, she almost never slept at the ranch. Her mother had a house in town, and Callie lived there. She spent a lot of time at the ranch, but we didn't really hang out."

Cort thought of his own dysfunctional family. "I guess what they say is true—you can pick your friends, but you can't pick your family."

"That's true. Maybe one day, when Callie has more perspective on life, we can be friends."

"I think your sister still has some growing up to do," Cort said. "But I don't think she's a lost cause."

Beside them, Minna and her companion stood up to leave. The younger woman gathered up their belongings, and Cort watched as the elderly lady carefully stretched her back, and then took a tentative step in the direction of the door. Alarmed by the number of obstacles that stood between her and the exit, Cort rose to his feet.

"Ma'am, would you allow a lowly cowboy to escort you to the door?" he asked gallantly, holding out an arm. "I'd consider it an honor."

To his surprise, Minna beamed up at him. "Young man, I would be delighted." She took his arm with a surprisingly strong grip as he steered her carefully between the tables. "I'm Minna Herdmann, and that's my great-granddaughter, Lynn."

"Pleased to meet you," he replied. "I'm Cort Channing."

"In town to escort Emma Claiborne to her sister's wedding, I hear. That's a fine mess, but even the darkest clouds have a silver lining." She cast him a shrewd look. "I'd suggest you tell that to your girl, but I get the feeling she'll figure it out sooner than later."

"Yes, ma'am," Cort said, completely baffled as to her meaning.

At the door, she released his arm and smiled at him again. "Thank you."

Her granddaughter hurried to take Minna's arm, and Cort held the door for them as they stepped outside, and made their way slowly down the sidewalk. He walked back to Emma, and sat down.

"She's a character," he said. "I like her."

"Most people do," Emma said, smiling. "That's why she practically gets her own holiday."

Their food arrived, and Cort looked with appreciation at the stack of potato pancakes and the side dish of homemade applesauce. He'd eaten breakfast at the house, but after Holt had started grilling him about his granddad's property, he'd stopped tasting anything. It bugged him that Holt knew about both the auction and the stud seed that would be included in the sale of the property. There was nothing he could do about it, however. He just had to trust that when the time came, he'd have enough money to override whatever offer Holt might throw on the table.

"C'mon, try them," Emma said. "It's the one thing I absolutely have to have whenever I come home. That, and anything from Rosa's Cantina."

Cort wondered if she was even aware that she referred to Last Stand as *home*. She'd done it several times, yet insisted she belonged in New York. But he'd never heard her call New York home. He forked a pancake onto his plate, and took an experimental mouthful. "You're right, these are delicious."

Emma smiled. "I thought you might like them."

"Emma Claiborne, as I live and breathe! Why, I haven't seen you in years!"

They both looked up to see a young woman standing near their table, staring at Emma with astonished delight. She was slender to the point of spindly, with blond hair that hung below her shoulders, and wide brown eyes. She wore pink medical scrubs and white sneakers, and some kind of ID badge around her neck.

"Jorie?"

"Yes! Oh my God, it's so good to see you again!"

Emma stood up, and the two women embraced.

"Here, ma'am, have a seat," Cort said, standing up to offer her a chair.

"Oh, no," she protested. "I can't stay. I have to be at the clinic in ten minutes, but I thought that was you and just wanted to come over and say hello."

"Do you work at the hospital?" Emma asked. "I remember you were always taking care of abandoned animals."

Jorie laughed and lifted her hands in surrender. "Still am! I work at the veterinary clinic as a vet tech, but I do wildlife rehab at my house in my spare time."

Cort remained standing, as his manners didn't allow him to sit while a woman was also standing. But when Jorie's eyes slid to him, Emma seemed to recollect herself.

"Jorie, this is my, uh, boyfriend, Cort Channing. Cort, this is Jorie Russell. We used to hang out together whenever I'd come home for the summer."

"It's nice to meet you, Cort. I wish I could stay, but I'll be late for work," Jorie explained, and then her eyes clouded. "I was worried about you when I heard Callie was marrying your ex, but it seems you're doing okay?"

Emma gave her a reassuring smile. "I'm doing great. They say everything happens for a reason, right?"

Cort didn't miss how Jorie's gaze flickered over him in shy admiration. "Well, I'd say it was for a very good reason."

The women embraced again, and then Jorie made her way to the door, waving to several other patrons on her way out.

"She seems nice," Cort said as they took their seats again.

"She is. She had a rough upbringing, but it never seemed to get her down. She's always upbeat, and she's always taking care of others."

"So how are you doing?" he asked gently. "You sounded pretty convincing when you said you were doing great."

She seemed to consider his words for a moment, and then shrugged. "I'm doing okay. Better than okay, actually. Things seem better this morning than they did last night. I still need to make my peace with Callie, but I won't force it until she's ready. Maybe in a few months, when the dust of the wedding has settled, we can talk."

"And Damon?"

"What about him?"

"Will you make your peace with him too?"

Cort didn't like the thought of Emma making any kind of peace with Damon Stewart. They had too much history together.

"I actually felt bad for him last night," she said. "He seemed a little pathetic, asking me to put in a good word for him with my family. I never really stopped to consider what it's been like for him. I guess I just assumed that everyone here welcomed their relationship with open arms."

"So you're not pining for him?"

Emma blinked. "Excuse me? *Pining* for him? Who even says that?"

Cort chuckled. "I do, apparently."

"No, I'm not *pining* for him." She was quiet for a moment, considering. "Our relationship had actually been strained for months before he finally ended it. At the time, I didn't realize it was because he was already in love with Callie—and I do think he is. In love with her, I mean."

"Well, I hope it works out for them." He gave her a half smile. "For everyone's sake."

When they had finished their meal, they left the restaurant and strolled along the covered sidewalk until they reached the post office. Cort waited while Emmaline collected her package, which was easily four feet wide and just as high.

"Is that one of your paintings?" he asked.

"Yes. I remember that Callie really liked it."

"That's pretty generous of you," Cort observed. "Most people in your place would have given them a toaster."

"Maybe I should just send them a thank-you note, instead."

"There's an idea," Cort replied, but thought maybe he should be the one to send the card.

As he carried the painting back to the truck, he was glad for his dark sunglasses, which hid the fact he was completely ogling the gentle swing of Emmaline's hips as she strode along the sidewalk in front of him. She might not believe she belonged here in Texas, but Cort had never seen anyone look more at home than Emmaline Claiborne did as she walked along Main Street in Last Stand.

⚔

THE DRAGONFLY WAS a farm-to-table restaurant built on stilts overlooking the river. Gus had reserved the outside deck for the rehearsal dinner. The building was a rustic, post-and-beam structure with wide plank flooring, wooden walls, and soaring overhead beams which had been wrapped in mini-lights.

The outside deck had a sailcloth canopy to protect diners

from the sun and elements. A dozen tables had been arranged around the perimeter of the space and covered in white floor-length tablecloths with fresh greenery and tiny votive centerpieces. A three-piece jazz ensemble had set up near the entrance to the deck, allowing both the indoor and outdoor guests to enjoy the music.

Emma had said the dinner would be a small gathering, but Cort estimated there were at least forty people already there, enjoying cocktails and appetizers on the expansive deck. He recognized many of them from the previous night at the Claiborne house. Emma put her arm through his, and leaned into him.

"This restaurant is owned by Delilah Corbyn. Her mother owns the Western store where we bought our boots this morning," Emmaline told him.

"I'm impressed."

"Delilah is the chef. I've never eaten here, but I've heard her food is incredible. Everything is locally sourced."

Suddenly, a child disengaged herself from a group of adults and ran across the deck toward him. Cort recognized Lucy Becker scant seconds before she threw her little arms around his waist and hugged him. He looked helplessly at Emmaline, and then grinned and patted the child's hair. She tipped her face up and looked at him.

"Thank you for saving me, Mr. Channing," she said, and smiled, revealing an adorable gap in her teeth. Cort felt something tighten in his chest. She looked nothing like the pale, waxen corpse he'd fished out of the river the previous night. Now her hair was shiny and bouncy and tied back with a ribbon, her cheeks were pink, and her blue eyes sparkled with childish delight.

Cort was only vaguely aware that people had stopped talking, and had turned to watch the exchange. Carefully disengaging himself from the child's clinging arms, he crouched on the balls of his feet until he was on eye level with her.

"Miss Lucy," he said gravely, "I'm so glad you're here tonight. You sure do look pretty. I wonder if you might save a dance for me later on?"

"I can only stay until nine o'clock, because Momma says I'm already up way past my bedtime. I'm Callie's flower girl, and tomorrow is a big day."

"It sure is," Cort agreed. "But you can't go home without promising me that dance."

Lucy flushed with pleasure. "Okay," she agreed. "But I have to ask my momma first."

"Absolutely," Cort said.

"I think we can stay long enough for you to dance with Mr. Channing," replied Christine, who had come to stand beside her daughter. Cort stood up, unprepared when Christine stepped forward and hugged him, hard. "Thank you," she said fiercely. "You saved my baby girl."

A young bearded man stood beside Christine, and now he held out his hand. "I'm Lucy's father, Keith Becker. I don't know how to thank you for what you did last night."

"I'm just glad she's okay," Cort said gruffly.

"She came home this morning, and it's like nothing ever happened," Christine said. "I'm not even sure she remembers anything. We're so grateful."

Someone pressed a drink into his hand, and Cort realized the other guests were all standing and holding drink glasses.

"I'd like to propose a toast," Keith said, raising his own glass. "To Cort Channing. Thank you for saving my daughter's life. We will forever be grateful. If we can't pay it back somehow, we'll be sure to pay it forward."

"Hear, hear!"

Cort touched his glass to Keith's, feeling both embarrassed and moved by the gesture. As he took a swallow of the drink, his eyes met Emma's. She was looking at him as if he really was some kind of hero. For the next thirty minutes, until they finally sat down to eat, Cort found himself besieged by well-wishers and people who wanted to thank him for rescuing Lucy. He wasn't unaccustomed to attention—as a bull rider, he engaged with his fans on a regular basis—but this was different. This felt personal. Even Callie's mother, Rachel Dean, had made a point of coming over to speak with him, and express her appreciation for what he'd done.

He wondered how they would feel if they knew the truth about him—that he was the son of a serial con man who had swindled at least three women out of their life savings. Roy Channing hadn't even married Cort's mother, at least not legally. He'd been married to another woman when he'd walked down the aisle with Bobbi Walker. Even the media hadn't yet uncovered his past, but that would change if he rose high enough in the bull riding ranks. He dreaded that day almost as much as he welcomed it. Having the truth out in the open would be a relief to him. Maybe it wouldn't eliminate the shame and guilt he lived with on a nearly daily basis, but at least he'd no longer feel the need to hide from his past.

"You're the star of the show tonight." Emma smiled at him as they made their way toward the tables.

"I don't feel right about that," Cort said. "This is Callie's special weekend, and I can't help but feel like I hijacked it."

Emma made a sound of dismissal. "You didn't hijack it, Cort, you saved it. If you hadn't been there to pull Lucy out of the river, the wedding would have been called off, and there would be no special weekend. She should be thanking you."

Cort hadn't been the only one to notice that both Callie and Damon seemed to be avoiding him and Emma. Cort hadn't missed how first Gus, and then Holt, had pulled Callie aside to speak privately with her. Both times, her gaze had traveled to where he and Emma stood, and he knew they were probably encouraging her to come over and speak to them. But she'd remained stubbornly surrounded by her friends, refusing to either acknowledge or approach them. He also knew Emma wasn't as unaffected by her sister's aloof attitude as she pretended to be. She'd already had two drinks, and when she thought nobody was looking, her eyes lingered on her sister, her brow furrowed.

"Honey, maybe you should slow down a bit," Cort cautioned as she ordered a third glass of wine. She wouldn't thank him if he had to carry her out to the truck later because she was too drunk to walk on her own. "You haven't had anything to eat since this morning."

"I'm fine," she said with a bright smile. "Besides, the wine is grown locally by August Wolf. It would be rude to not drink it."

"Is he here tonight?" Cort asked.

"Nope, don't think so," she said happily. "Oh, they're serving dinner!"

They had been seated at a table with Gus, Rosa-Maria, Holt, Evan, and Jessie Montero and her father, Jose. As Emma had predicted, the food was delicious, and Cort thought he'd never had filet mignon as tender or flavorful. During the meal, Gus stood up and went over to stand behind Callie and Damon as he made a brief, congratulatory toast to the couple. After he sat down, Damon's father made a similar toast, but Cort noticed how Damon's mother watched Emma with an expression that was both compassionate and concerned.

Damon and Callie presented the bridesmaids and groomsmen with small gifts, and then Callie thanked her parents for everything they had done in helping pull the wedding together. A waiter wheeled out the groom's cake, a three-tiered cake cleverly designed to look like three stacks of Damon's bestselling espionage books, much to everyone's delight. Cort glanced over at Emmaline. She had a smile pasted on her face, but he knew her well enough to see the small signs of her distress, like the way she was wringing the life out of her cloth napkin, and the rapid rise and fall of her chest as her breathing quickened. As they cut the cake and began serving it, Cort stood up and reached down for

Emma's hand.

"Dance with me, honey. They're playing a slow song."

Emma looked up at him, and for just a moment, he thought she would refuse.

"Alright, cowboy." She stood up, wobbling a little in her heels. She wore a deep red sleeveless dress that cinched in around her waist, and emphasized the curve of her breasts and hips. She'd left her hair partially down, so that a heavy lock fell forward over her shoulder. She bent down to adjust a strap on her sandals, and Cort saw the dress had a long zip down the back, the kind a man could undo in one fluid movement. The kind of dress that would just slide off…

She straightened and smiled at him, and he had to shake the lecherous thoughts away. Her eyes had the soft, unfocused look of someone who'd imbibed a little too much.

"You doing okay, honey?" he asked, as he drew her into the curve of his body, sliding one hand to the small of her back, and curling his other hand around her fingers. She fit neatly against him, and he breathed in the fragrance that he'd come to associate with her. He moved her easily around the small dance floor, their bodies in perfect rhythm.

"Doing just fine," she murmured, and slid her free arm over his shoulder to press her fingers against the back of his neck. "But I'll admit, I can't wait for this night to be over."

"We'll leave soon," he promised.

"You look nice tonight, by the way."

"Oh yeah? You look nice too. That color is real pretty on you."

She leaned back against his arm to look at him. He wore

179

a white Western shirt with mother-of-pearl snap buttons and a silver bolo tie, and good Wranglers paired with the championship belt buckle he'd won at his first semi-pro bull riding event. He had other buckles, but none that meant as much to him as this one.

"Why are you always so nice to me?" she asked.

"Why wouldn't I be?" he asked, chuckling. "You're easy to be nice to."

The music swelled to a crescendo before it began to ebb, and Cort dipped Emma dramatically over his arm so that she gave a startled laugh and clutched at his shoulder. She was still laughing as he swung her back to an upright position.

"Cort Channing," she gasped when she could finally speak. "I was not expecting that! I almost ended up on the floor."

"I'd never let you fall," he said.

She didn't release him, and for a moment, they stood locked together, staring at each other as her laughter faded. Emma's gaze drifted to his mouth, and her lips parted in what seemed like an invitation. Cort began to bend his head when someone tapped him on his shoulder.

"Excuse me. Could I cut in and have the next dance with this beautiful young lady?"

Gus Claiborne stood watching them, humor sparkling in his blue eyes. Reluctantly, Cort released Emma. "Of course, sir. I believe I owe another young lady a dance before her momma whisks her away to bed."

He handed Emma off to her father, and went in search of little Lucy, letting her stand on the toes of his new boots as he carefully twirled her around the dance floor. Other couples joined them, and although Cort listened with apparent attention to Lucy's endless chatter, his gaze was drawn repeatedly to Emma as she danced with Gus.

"Your girlfriend is pretty," Lucy said.

"I think so too. Almost as pretty as you are."

Lucy grinned. "Are you going to marry her?"

"I don't know. I haven't asked her."

"My mommy said she and Callie are in a fight, and that makes Callie sad."

"Well," Cort said carefully, "sometimes sisters don't always get along. But that doesn't mean they don't still love each other. I know Emma loves Callie."

"Sometimes me and my brother fight," Lucy admitted. "But he tried to save me last night, before you came, so I know he really loves me."

"I'm sure he does, sweetheart."

The music ended, and Cort returned Lucy to her mother, who thanked him yet again before bundling the little girl off. He was just moving to intercept Emma as she returned to the table when he felt a light hand on his arm. Turning, he found himself face-to-face with Callie. Her astonishing blue eyes were guarded, as if she expected him to rebuff her. Up close, she looked much younger than twenty-five, and he thought he detected shadows under her eyes.

"Ma'am," he said, and touched the brim of his hat.

"I just wanted to say thank you for what you did last night," she said stiffly.

"Anyone else would have done the same," he assured her.

"Do you love her?"

"Beg your pardon?"

"Do you love my sister?" she demanded, her tone bordering on hostile. Several people moved closer, listening with avid expressions to the unfolding drama. Then Emma was there, sliding a hand through his arm.

"What's going on?" she asked.

Callie swung her attention to Emma. "Are you two really serious about each other? Is that what you want us to believe?"

Cort felt Emma stiffen. "What's it to you? Our business is just that—our business. Or did you want to have a go at my current boyfriend too?"

Callie gasped, and her face blanched beneath the abundance of freckles.

Damon approached, giving Emma and Cort an apologetic smile before he tried to draw Callie away. "Sweetheart," he said carefully, as if speaking to a child, "this isn't the time or place." He lowered his voice. "Please don't make a scene."

"I'm just trying to understand what's going on here," Callie said, pushing him away. "Everyone thinks my sister is so perfect. Well, I know better."

"What are you talking about?" Emma demanded. "Stop this, Callie, you're making a spectacle of yourself."

"Callie, darlin', why don't you sit down and let your guests enjoy the rest of the evening?" Gus suggested.

"I found this on the internet," Callie said triumphantly, and held up her mobile phone. "It's a video of Cort Channing at the rodeo in New York three weeks ago." She turned the screen toward them and increased the volume. "After his ride, he threw his hat to Emma while she sat in the stands and here he is, telling a reporter *that he only met her a couple of days earlier.*"

"Callie," Emma said quietly. "Why are you doing this?"

"No, Emma," Callie retorted. "Why are *you* doing this? Why would you bring some stranger to our house and try to foist him off as your boyfriend?"

"You really want to know why?" Emma snapped, her patience evaporating. "Because I knew you would do something just like this. You'd try to humiliate me in front of everyone and make me feel like a loser because you've always needed to compete with me. I knew if I came back alone, you'd never let me forget how you *won*. How you stole my boyfriend and—"

"I didn't *steal* him," Callie protested. "He never loved you; he just didn't know how to tell you."

"Well, thank you for that," Emma said, her tone biting. "I guess you both did me a favor. Now if you don't mind, I'm going to take my fake boyfriend—who, by the way, has been more of a real boyfriend to me than Damon ever was— and go home. I hope you're both very happy together."

Cort watched the scene unfold in stunned silence. He wouldn't have been able to intervene if his life had depended on it. He'd never seen Emma so fierce, and quite frankly, her last statement left him feeling dumbfounded. All he could think was that if what she'd said was true and he'd been more of a boyfriend to her than Damon had been, then Damon really was an idiot.

"Ma'am," he said politely to Callie, and touched the brim of his hat once more before guiding Emma from the restaurant with a hand at the small of her back. He was only vaguely aware of the commotion that erupted behind them, but he distinctly heard Gus's booming voice demanding to know what in Sam hell that had been about. Later, they would explain to him why they'd done what they had, but right now Cort's only concern was getting Emma as far away from the gathering as possible.

They walked to the pickup truck in silence, and as Cort opened the passenger door to help Emma climb into the cab, she turned to him. Her face was a pale oval in the indistinct light of the parking lot, her eyes dark and searching.

"I'm sorry," she said, her voice earnest. "I'm sorry I dragged you into this. But I want you to know I meant every word I said."

Then she flung her arms around his neck and kissed him.

Chapter Twelve

HER MOUTH MOVED hungrily against his, and for just an instant, Cort was too stunned to respond. Then sensation crashed over him. Her pillowy lips fastened over his own, and her soft, hot tongue pressed into his mouth. He tasted wine and *her*, and he was lost. He couldn't have done anything to resist her, even if he'd wanted to. With a muffled groan, he slid his hands to her sweet bottom and lifted her onto the passenger seat. He kissed her back, longer and deeper, as she speared her fingers through his hair, knocking his hat to the ground.

Cort stepped between her splayed thighs, his hands roaming over her body, his fingers brushing over the zipper at the back of her dress. He didn't give in to temptation, and instead cupped her bottom and pulled her to the very edge of the leather seat, until her skirt pushed up over her thighs, and he was pressed against her center. Emmaline made a soft, moaning sound and dragged her lips from his.

"Cort," she said, her breath coming in fitful pants. "Please, take me somewhere, anywhere."

"You sure about this, honey?" he asked, and raised a hand to her face to cup the curve of her cheek, brushing his thumb over the softness of her skin. "There're things you don't know about me."

"I know all I need to know," she breathed, "and I meant what I said back there. These past two days with you have been better for me than the entire three years I spent with *him*. Please, Cort, I want you so much."

"Where should we go?"

"Home," she said. "Take me home."

Carefully, he stepped back and pulled her dress down over her legs before scooping his hat from the ground, and closing her door. He rounded the hood of the truck, knowing he had no right to take Emmaline Claiborne to bed, but knowing he would anyway. They made the drive back to Riverrun Ranch in silence except for the soft music on the radio. Cort kept his fingers laced with hers the whole way.

The house was dark and silent as they made their way up the stairs to Emmaline's bedroom. As soon as he closed the door behind them, she turned into his arms. Cort tossed his hat onto the nearby chair and drew her close. She was like a flame, and his body burned wherever she touched him. He cupped her face, tenderly cradling her jaw in his hands as he lowered his head and kissed her. The hot silk of her tongue slid sensuously against his, but he wanted more. He deepened the kiss, his whole body aching and hard. She clutched at him, her fingers digging into the muscles of his back as she sought to get closer still. Darkness wrapped around them, cool and sheltering, as Emmaline unfastened his bolo tie and dragged his shirt from the waistband. Then she pushed her hands under the fabric and slid her fingers over his heated skin.

"Take this off," she pleaded against his mouth.

Her fingers came around to the front of his shirt, searching for the buttons. They came free with a *pop-pop-pop*, and then her palms were exploring the contours of his stomach and chest. Cort's muscles contracted and behind the restraint of his zipper, he swelled even more. When the shirt finally hung open, Emmaline pressed her mouth against his skin. He shivered as she pressed hot, moist kisses against his abdomen, and then moved upward to nibble and kiss his chest. Cort kept his hands lightly on her head, his fingers sifting through her soft hair to trace the delicate whorl of her ears, and massage the tender skin beneath.

But when her fingers moved to his belt, he swept her into his arms, ignoring her surprised cry as he carried her over to the bed. Laying her across the coverlet, he eased himself down beside her and kissed her again. She sighed into his mouth and turned into him. Cort slid an arm beneath her and as they kissed, he used his free hand to explore her curves, stroking over her breasts and hip, and lower to the hem of her dress. He eased it upward and smoothed his palm over her thighs. Emmaline shifted restlessly and her legs fell open. Cort cupped her intimately, until she arched into his hand.

"Take these off," she begged against his lips, and her hand went again to his belt buckle.

"There's no rush, honey," he said, and began to massage her soft, feminine folds through the silk of her panties. She made a stifled moaning sound and his fingers grew damp as he stroked her. "Does that feel good?"

"Yes," she gasped. "Please, Cort…"

Removing his hand, he turned her so that he could reach the zipper at the back of her dress, pulling it downward in one smooth movement. He tugged the fabric down, and Emmaline slid her arms free. Beneath the dress, she wore a lacy black bra. Cort stroked his fingers over one breast, and then the other, gently cupping and squeezing the creamy mounds until her breath quickened, and she arched beneath him. Dipping his head, he drew one nipple into his mouth, drawing on her through the insubstantial material of the bra, before he reached behind her and unfastened the clasp. He pulled the bra free and dropped it onto the floor before he bent his attention back to her breasts, laving one and then the other with his tongue, while Emma clutched his head and arched upward.

"Is that good?" he asked, his voice rough against her skin.

She made an inarticulate sound of assent, and Cort pushed the dress further down, past her hips. Emmaline helped him, wriggling the dress down her legs until she could kick it free, until only her black panties and her heeled sandals remained.

Freeing his arm, Cort pressed his mouth against her ribs, tasting her skin as he worked his way down the length of her body. He paused over the small whorl of her navel, teasing it with his tongue, until he continued his downward path. When he reached the edge of her panties, he slid a finger inside the elastic band, but made no attempt to remove them. Glancing up, he saw Emmaline watching him intently.

Kneeling between her splayed thighs, he lifted one foot and carefully undid the tiny buckle on her sandal before removing it. He kissed her ankle and the arch of her foot before he did the same with her other foot. Only then did he unfasten the heavy buckle on his belt, sliding it off and letting it drop to the floor. He released the button on his jeans and slid his zipper partially down, but only to relieve some of the pressure.

Emmaline lifted one foot and placed it on his thigh, her painted toes curling into the fabric of his jeans. Cort lifted her leg in his hands and skated his mouth across the smooth, silken skin, starting at her ankle and moving upward until he reached her inner thigh. He heard her swift, indrawn breath as he nibbled gently, and then soothed the area with his tongue. He was fiercely aroused, his body hammering at him to take what she offered. He wanted badly to be inside her, but he forced himself to go slow, to make this last, because he'd thought of little else during the last twenty-four hours, and he didn't want this to end. He also wasn't sure Emma was completely sober, which was another consideration, one he didn't want to think about. He just wanted to make this good for her.

"Tell me what you want, honey," he murmured against her skin.

EMMA HAD GONE too long without intimacy of any kind, and beneath Cort's skillful mouth and hands, her body thrummed with pleasure and unfulfilled need. The sensation of his lips against the sensitive skin of her inner thigh caused her to shiver. She could feel the scrape of his beard growth and, combined with the heat of his breath, it was all she could do not to beg him to take her fast and hard and endlessly.

"I just want you," she managed to gasp. "Now."

But Cort only renewed his attention to her leg, gently biting the inside of her knee before he lowered her foot back to the mattress. His shirt hung open, and in the dim light that filtered through the window, Emma could see the hard muscles of his abdomen and the flat planes of his chest. She wanted to touch him, explore him, spend hours learning the contours of his body.

"Soon, baby," he promised, and his deep voice sounded husky, sending new shivers of anticipation through her.

She watched as he tugged her panties down over her hips, pulling them free from her legs until there was nothing more to hide her from his view. The knowledge that she was completely naked to his glittering gaze while he remained almost completely dressed excited her beyond reason. She lay before him like a pagan offering, willing him to worship her.

Bending forward, Cort braced his hands on either side of her and pressed his mouth against her stomach. Her muscles contracted, and her breasts rose and fell with her agitated breathing. He glanced up at her over the length of her body, and Emma saw heat and intent in his green eyes. Slowly, he dipped his head and nuzzled his face into the vee of her thighs, before sliding his big hand along the inside of her leg, and opening her wide.

"No, Cort, wait—" she protested, and pushed futilely at his head.

"Why?" Without waiting for her response, he put his mouth on her, his tongue parting her and licking at the place where she pulsed and ached.

"Oh…" she moaned, and put her hands over her face, mortified. Somehow, this seemed even more intimate than actual sex. But then pleasure speared through her, and any embarrassment was forgotten as he draped her legs over his shoulders, and used his mouth to drive her wild, licking her aroused flesh in erotic swirls. Emma's heartbeat pounded hard behind her ribs, and she struggled for breath, gasping Cort's name. But when he slid a finger inside her, a groan escaped her and her hips lifted helplessly, even as her fingers clenched in his hair.

Pressure gathered and coiled, tighter and harder, like a clock spring that had been overwound. Emma heard the sounds that escaped her, desperate gasps and groans that she was helpless to prevent. They seemed to encourage Cort, who inserted a second finger, stretching and filling her, before he began a slow, steady glide, in and out. Emma's inner muscles contracted, clenching around his fingers as tension drew her tight. All the while, his mouth tormented the small, aching nub, flicking steadily until the pressure suddenly shattered. Emma cried out as her back bowed off the bed and she was lost in a series of hard, shuddering spasms. She rode the intense pleasure as Cort continued to play with her, softening his mouth to wring every last twitch and tremor from her.

Only when she lay drained and unmoving, her limbs splayed out in sated abandon, did he withdraw. He eased himself up beside her before pulling her into the strong circle of his arms, holding her tightly as his mouth pressed kisses over her eyes, her cheeks and, finally, her lips. Emma moved one hand to his waistband, and the hard rise of flesh beneath the half-opened zipper.

"Take these off," she murmured against his mouth.

"That's enough for tonight, honey," he said, covering her exploring hand, and moving it away from his body. "Your family is going to return soon. Besides, you've had an emotional day and a little too much wine."

"I'm not drunk," she protested. "I want you to make love to me all the way."

"I will," he promised. "But not tonight. We have too much to sort out, and I won't be able to look your father in the eye tomorrow when he asks if I've taken advantage of you."

"He won't. He doesn't care. He even said we're both consenting adults."

Cort made a sound that was half laugh, half groan. "That was when he believed we were a real couple."

"Aren't we a real couple?" she asked. "That felt real to me."

"It was more real than you know," Cort assured her. "But if we're going to be a real couple, there are things you need to know about me first, things I need to tell you and your family."

"Tell me now," she said, hugging him tighter, but she couldn't prevent a yawn that nearly split her jaw. She felt tired and replete all the way to her bones, but this was important. She wanted a relationship with Cort more than she'd wanted anything in a very long time. But she had the frightening sense that if she let him go now, she might lose him. "Take off your clothes, come to bed, and tell me."

Cort kissed her sweetly before he used the back of his fingers to brush a lock of hair away from her face. "Get some sleep, honey. Tomorrow is another day. We'll figure this out when you're not so tired."

Rolling off the bed, he helped her climb under the covers, tucking them securely around her shoulders before he buttoned his shirt, and then fished around on the floor for his belt.

"Where are you going?" Emma asked, and raised herself on one elbow as an alarming thought occurred to her. "You're not leaving Riverrun, are you?"

"Not a chance. I'm going to sleep in the bunkhouse tonight. Considering what happened at the Dragonfly, I figure your brothers already want to kick my ass, so there's no point in antagonizing them further by sleeping here."

"I wish you'd stay," she begged.

But Cort only kissed her again. "Sweet dreams, darlin'."

He let himself out of her bedroom, closing the door quietly behind him. Emma lay in the darkness, listening to his footfalls as he descended the stairs, and then she heard the distant closing of the front door. She got up and used the bathroom, and then pulled on a pair of pajamas before she climbed back into bed. She bunched the pillow beneath her cheek and replayed the events of the night in her mind. And when finally, she heard her father and brothers return to the house, she decided it didn't matter how long she'd known Cort...three days, three weeks, or three years. She felt she knew him better than she'd ever known Damon. And whatever it was he thought he needed to tell her about himself and his past, it wouldn't matter to her.

She was falling in love with him.

Chapter Thirteen

A s the weatherman had promised, the day of the wedding dawned clear and cloudless, and service vehicles began rolling down the long driveway before Emma was even out of bed. Through the window near the headboard, she watched as florists and musicians and caterers made the final preparations for the big event. Emma wished she could pull the covers back over her head and sleep until the following day. Voices drifted up from downstairs, and although she could make out her father's deep voice and those of her brothers, the words themselves were indistinct.

Was Cort with them? The thought that he might be facing all that Claiborne testosterone without her to support him made her sit up and throw her covers off. Sunlight filtered in through the sheers, revealing what the cover of nightfall had hidden. Her black bra and panties lay on the floor next to her sandals. And the red dress—the one she'd bought for a long-ago evening with Damon—lay crumpled at the foot of the bed, the gold zipper winking in the light.

Emma picked it up and smoothed the fabric over her arm. When she'd bought the dress, she'd hoped it would cause her date to look at her with longing and lust. Never in a million years would she have guessed that a rugged, sexy cowboy—a bull rider—would be the one to slowly peel the garment from her body, and then reduce to her to a mindless, quivering mass of nerve endings.

She collected the discarded undergarments and put them in the laundry bin, and then realized Cort's duffel bag was missing. She searched the room, but all of his belongings were gone. A small knot of anxiety settled in her stomach as she dressed quickly in a pair of shorts and a T-shirt, and made her way downstairs. The masculine voices were coming from behind her father's closed office door. Emma put a cautious ear against the panels, trying to decipher the conversation. The voices were low and fierce, and although she couldn't make out the words, she heard Cort's voice, smoky and deep amidst the angry baritones.

Without thinking, Emma opened the door. Four pairs of eyes turned to look at her, and she knew immediately that the day wasn't going to be nearly as sunny as the weatherman had predicted. Cort stood on one side of the room, still dressed in the white shirt he'd worn the night before, hands shoved deep into his pockets. Color rode high on his cheekbones, and his eyes glowed unnaturally bright. Even from across the room, Emma could feel the anger radiating off him.

Glancing at her brothers and her father, she could see Holt's fury level nearly matched Cort's, while Evan and her father seemed calmer, almost as if they were observers and not really involved in whatever was going down in front of them.

"What's going on?" Closing the door behind her, she stepped deeper into the room.

"Nothing, honey," Cort said, and his face softened when he looked at her. "We're just talking."

Glancing at Holt's face, Emma saw him struggling to contain his emotions, which made her feel scared. Holt never lost his temper, and never let emotions rule him. He was the epitome of the word *control*, and seeing him on the edge of his composure caused alarm bells to go off in her head.

"What are you talking about?" she asked, and her gaze slid to her father and Evan.

Her father's face looked almost sad, as if he was wondering how to tell her that her dog had died, while Evan crossed his arms and looked pointedly at his feet. Evan, always irreverent and funny, could infuse humor into any situation, but clearly this one was an exception. He refused to meet her eyes.

"How did you meet Cort?" her father asked, his voice gentle.

"Why is that important?"

"Just answer me, darlin'," he said.

Emma glanced swiftly at Cort, and he gave her a brief nod. Why did they want to know? Had they discovered something about Cort that she didn't know? Something nefarious? A horrible thought occurred to her.

"Oh my God, you're married."

To her relief, Cort shook his head, and gave her a brief smile. "No, honey. I'm not married." He looked at Holt. "And I've never been married."

"So what is it, then?" She crossed the room to Cort's side and slid her hand through his arm, looking up at his closed face.

"How did you two meet?" her father asked again. "The real story, please."

"We met in a bar in Manhattan," Emma said. "I was waiting for someone else, but didn't know I was being stood up. Cort came in to tell me, and then gave me tickets to the bull riding event. So I went."

"And how did he know you were going to be at that bar?" Holt demanded. "How did he know you were being stood up?"

Emma frowned. "He's a friend of the guy I was supposed to meet. He knew his friend couldn't make it, so he came instead."

"Jesus Christ," Holt muttered. He gave Cort a scathing look. "Is that how it worked? Your friend would find women online, soften them up, and then pretend he couldn't meet them, so you could sweep in and scam them?"

"What are you talking about?" Emma demanded. "That's not what happened!"

"You know Cort looked at your online dating account, right?" Holt asked.

Emma shrugged. "I guess so. But only so he would know what I looked like when he came to tell me I was being stood up. What he did was both thoughtful and gentlemanly. I could have been sitting there all night, never knowing what had happened."

"Emma, this guy's been playing you all along. Has he

asked you for money yet? Told you he needs it to *buy back his granddad's ranch*?" Holt made air quotes with his fingers.

"No," Emma said, shocked. "He hasn't asked me for anything. Why would he? He has money saved, and he has a plan."

"Sure he does," Holt scoffed. "Just like his father did."

"What is he talking about?" she asked Cort, but his face remained shuttered, and he made no effort to defend himself against Holt's accusations.

"I did some checking into your fake boyfriend's background," Holt said.

"You did *what*?"

"Hank Walker is his granddad, like he said, but I'm betting he doesn't tell too many people who his father is." He threw a challenging glance at Cort. "Do you want to tell her, or should I?"

Cort looked at Emma, and his expression was one of weary resignation. "I never knew my father. He left when I was two years old. I've never had anything to do with him, and I have no idea where he is now." He switched his attention to Holt, and his mouth tilted in a sardonic smile. "Guess I don't have the kind of financial resources where I can hire an investigator to dig into people's personal affairs."

"Financial resources," Holt repeated softly. "And there's the crux of the whole issue. Bull riding isn't paying out as well as you'd hoped, and you're not getting any younger, so you thought maybe if you found yourself a vulnerable young woman from a wealthy family, you could coerce her into believing you cared about her, maybe even persuade her into lending you money. Isn't that right? Money you'd never need to pay her back, because you'd be long gone."

Emma stared in disbelief at her brother. "Have you completely lost your mind, Holt Claiborne? Since when did you start accusing guests in your own house of trying to scam you?"

"Not me," Holt said. "*You.*"

"Emma," Cort said. "I can explain."

DESPITE BEING RAISED on the Double U Ranch, the place had never truly felt like home. Cort wasn't even sure why he wanted the property so badly, except maybe because his granddad had always been so adamant that he'd never get his hands on it. Or maybe he wanted to prove to his granddad— and himself—that he wasn't like his father.

Cort had heard the story about his father more times than he cared to recall. His granddad had taken a perverse delight in telling Cort how Roy Channing had been a conman and a bigamist who had managed to convince at least three different women to marry him, before swindling them out of their money. Cort's mother, Bobbi, had been one of his victims.

By the time Hank Walker suspected Roy Channing wasn't all he claimed to be, Roy had vanished, taking more than twenty thousand dollars in cash, and a quarter of a million dollars' worth of Hank's prize bull seed with him. A tearful Bobbi had revealed that Roy had persuaded her to withdraw the money from the family safe, promising he would invest it and turn it into ten times its original worth. He hadn't told her he also intended to take the canisters of liquid nitrogen from the breeding barn, where the priceless seed straws were stored.

By the time her father realized what had happened, Roy Channing had disappeared from their lives.

Bobbi had been inconsolable, convinced Roy would never abandon her or their two-year-old son. Against her father's wishes, she spent two years looking for him. She'd finally tracked him to Nevada, only to find him married to another woman and living under a different name. On her way back to Texas, she must have fallen asleep at the wheel, because she'd driven her little Chevy sedan straight into the path of an oncoming eighteen-wheeler. At least, Cort *told* himself she'd fallen asleep. He couldn't—*wouldn't*—believe his mother had deliberately left him alone in the world with only a bitter, angry old man to raise him. The canisters of liquid nitrogen had never been recovered, and if Roy had told Bobbi what he'd done with them, she hadn't passed that information on to her father before she'd died. Hank Walker had never recovered from the loss, and his bull breeding business had gone into a decline the day he'd learned of his daughter's death.

Cort relayed the story as dispassionately as he could, but acknowledged it didn't look good for him. But how to convince the Claiborne men that it had been Emma's photo on the dating app that had reached something deep inside him, and not her connections to the wealthy Germaine family, or the Claiborne money?

There'd be no way he'd ever ask for a handout, and he would never, *ever* use a woman that way. He'd earn his money the hard way—on the back of a bull—or he'd go without. Now he finished his story and looked at Emma, trying to gauge her reaction.

"So that's it?" she asked, and swung her gaze to her brothers and her father. "You're condemning him based on his father's actions? Cort was little more than a baby when that happened! He doesn't even know his father!"

"We all know the apple doesn't fall far from the tree, and Roy Channing—his father—was a conman, Emma," Holt said patiently. "The way Cort inveigled himself into your life—into our lives—is a classic swindler move. Part of the whole persona is knowing how to act trustworthy and innocent, like he's the victim and not you. Christ, even his own granddad didn't trust him. Otherwise he'd have made provisions for him in his will. Instead, he drove the Double U Ranch into the ground rather than let his grandson have one red cent from it. What does that tell you?"

"That maybe he was just a bitter old man, grieving for his daughter, and suffering from dementia." She looked up at Cort. "I trust you, Cort."

Her expression was so determinedly supportive that Cort felt his chest tighten. He'd been wrong to accompany her to Last Stand; he saw that now. No matter how mistaken Holt was about his motives, or how much the ugly accusations cut him to the quick, it wasn't worth driving a wedge between Emmaline and her family. If his father's actions had taught him one thing, it was the importance of a family that loved and supported you. He'd never had that.

"Listen, honey," he said gently, and brushed the backs of his fingers along her cheek. "I'm going to head out. You're strong, and you're going to get through today and whatever happens afterward."

"No—"

"Shh. You can't persuade me on this, Emmaline. I'm not going to come between you and your family, but you should know I don't regret meeting you." He searched her eyes, letting her see the truth. "I don't regret any of it."

"You can't just leave, Cort." Her voice rose, and he could see tears threatening. "I won't let my family decide who I can and can't see. I'm a grown woman, and I get to decide. I want *you*."

Cort steeled himself against the pleading in her eyes. He had to leave before she started to cry. He could handle pretty much anything, but he didn't think he could stand Emmaline's tears. He had to leave now, or he was going to do something he'd regret, like beg Holt to reconsider and let him stay. Or punch him in the face. Neither would endear him to the other man.

"Let him go, Emmaline," said Gus. Stepping forward, he extended a hand toward Cort. "I wish we could have met under different circumstances, Cort Channing. For what it's worth, I'm not in favor of you leaving. I don't hold with judging a man by the actions of his father. If the Claibornes had been held to that standard, we'd have been run out of Texas generations ago."

Cort shook the older man's hand, and then turned to Emmaline, pointedly ignoring both Holt and Evan. "Walk me out, honey."

Her face began to crumple, and she turned toward her oldest brother. "Holt Claiborne, I will never forgive you for this. I thought I knew what betrayal felt like when Callie ran off with Damon. But what you're doing right now is even worse."

Cort saw Holt go a little pale beneath his tan, but his mouth flattened into a thin line, and his blue eyes grew hard. "One day, you'll thank me for it."

Emma gave a disbelieving laugh that ended on a choked sob, but she let Cort put his arm around her shoulders and lead her to the door. They walked onto the porch, where he'd left his duffel bag. He turned to face Emma, putting his arms around her and pulling her into his embrace. She smelled so good, felt so right in his arms, that his heart clenched hard. He might never have this again.

"Cort," she said, and then pressed her face against his chest, her hands fisting in his shirt. "This is so ridiculous, all of it. *Please* stay. Or tell me to come with you, and I will."

Cort used one finger to lift her chin, forcing her to look at him. "I have to go, and you shouldn't come with me. But after I buy back my granddad's ranch, you can bet I'll be back. Wherever you are, Emmaline, I'll find you."

"What about the Fourth of July rodeo here in Last Stand?" she asked. "Will I see you there?"

"I don't know," he said. "I think it's better if I just keep moving on. I don't want your family any more upset than they already are." He tipped his head and looked directly into her eyes. "Family is important, Emmaline, and yours loves you very much. Whatever you may think, you belong here."

"If you don't come back, Cort Channing," she said as tears filled her eyes, "I will never forgive you."

Cort searched her eyes, wanting to tell her so much, but knowing he had no right. Finally, he cradled her face in his hands and kissed her as sweetly as he knew how, pouring everything he felt for her into that single kiss. When he released her, she swayed a little and then regained her balance before wrapping her arms around her middle. He picked up his duffel bag and slung it over his shoulder, and looked at her for one long, last moment, imprinting her on his memory. Imprinting her on his heart. Then he turned and walked down the long driveway to the main road.

He didn't look back.

Chapter Fourteen

THE WEDDING GUESTS had assembled on the lawn, where more than four hundred white cloth-covered chairs had been carefully arranged. The pastor stood waiting beneath an arched trellis trimmed with flowers, overlooking the river. The musical ensemble played lovely, classical music that drifted through the air, carried on the warm breezes. On the terrace behind the house, the six bridesmaids and little Lucy waited for their cue, dressed in deep rose-colored gowns and clutching posies of white gardenias and lilies of the valley.

Inside the wedding tent, waitstaff popped bottles of champagne and dumped more ice over the troughs of bottled alcohol—everything from wine, beer, and hard cider to fruity wine coolers. The Henderson brothers had fired up their enormous grills several hours earlier, and the tantalizing aromas of barbequed beef, chicken, and pork permeated the air, making the guests anxious to get the vows over with so they could commence with the best part of the festivities.

Inside the house, Emma put the finishing touches on her makeup. Looking in the mirror, she thought no amount of cosmetics could hide the fact that she had spent most of the morning in tears. Outside her bedroom door, she could hear the hurried footsteps of people as they went back and forth, and up and down the stairs. Glancing at her bedside clock, she wondered why anyone was still in the house. She'd deliberately taken longer than necessary with her hair and makeup so that she would miss the actual exchange of vows. Not because she still had any feelings for Damon, but because she didn't think she could be happy for her sister after the way she'd humiliated Emma at the rehearsal dinner. If not for Callie, Holt never would have investigated Cort's background, and Cort might still be here at Riverrun with her.

A soft knock at her door startled her. "Come in," she called.

The door opened, and Rachel Dean poked her head through the opening. She looked stunning in a gown of spring green, embellished with tiny seed pearls. Her bright hair had been artfully arranged, and delicate gold earrings swung from her ears. Emma couldn't have been more surprised.

"Rachel," she said, her voice stiff. "I thought you would already be seated. Is everything okay?"

The older woman came into the room and carefully closed the door behind her. "Can I talk with you?"

Emma didn't know what to say, so she nodded, and gestured toward the two slipper chairs at the end of the bed. When Rachel had taken a seat, Emma sat across from her, thinking the other woman probably wanted to defend her daughter, or warn Emma about making a scene at the wedding. Anything to ensure Callie had her perfect day.

"I'll just get right to the point," Rachel said. "I don't condone what Callie and Damon did, but now that they're getting married, I hope you can forgive them both. Callie is your sister, after all."

Emma sighed. She'd been right. Rachel was only interested in making sure Emma wouldn't cause a fuss. "I'm over it, Rachel, really. I don't know if I can forgive them, but you don't need to worry that I'm going to humiliate Callie on her wedding day, the way she humiliated me last night."

"That was unforgivable," Rachel said quietly. "You're an adult and your relationships are your own business. You have the right to bring whomever you choose to the wedding. I'm sorry she did that to you, to both of you."

For a moment, Emma was too surprised to speak.

"I heard Cort left," Rachel continued. "I think Callie owes you an apology for that, as well."

Emma gave a bitter laugh. "We both know that's never going to happen. I had no idea she hates me so much."

"Oh, no, that's where you're wrong," Rachel said, her voice earnest. "Callie adores you, but she struggles with feelings of inadequacy because…well, because she was born out of wedlock. She resents the fact that your father and I never married. In her mind, you have what she's always wanted—legitimacy."

"But Daddy loves her as much as he does the rest of us," Emma protested. "He's never denied her anything."

"Except his name. She's not a Claiborne."

Emma thought of her own mother, and how she'd insisted that Emma wasn't a Claiborne, either. "Family is more than just a name," she said, realizing it was the truth. "It's about who stands by you when you need them most, and my father—her father—has always been there for her."

Rachel sighed. "She thinks because we never married that she's somehow less of a Claiborne. I've tried to explain to her that what happened between me and Gus all those years ago was a mistake, except for the fact that it resulted in her birth. It was a single night of bad judgment, during a time when your father and I were both feeling lonely and vulnerable. We might have been able to forget it had ever happened, except I ended up pregnant with Callie."

Emma narrowed her eyes at Rachel. "You didn't have a long-term affair with my father?"

Rachel closed her eyes briefly, and then looked directly at Emma. "No, it was nothing like that. Your father and I had been friends since childhood, but we crossed the line one night, and only one night. We managed to salvage our friendship, but there's never been anything romantic be-tween us." She was quiet for a long moment. "I've always carried the guilt of having ruined his marriage to your mother. Believe me, that was never my intention."

"Thank you for telling me that," Emma said. "All these years, I thought you were in love with my father, and that you would have done anything to be with him. My mother believed that too."

Rachel gave a rueful laugh. "We would have killed each other within the first year. We're good friends, but that's it." She pushed to her feet. "I just didn't want you to think that I had deliberately come between Gus and your mother. I never meant to hurt anyone. I just thought you should know."

"Thank you," Emma said.

Rachel paused with her hand on the doorknob. "Callie is young and she's headstrong, and I'm afraid I've spoiled her. She doesn't like hearing the word *no*, and she's happiest when she's the center of attention. That's no excuse for her behavior, but maybe it explains it a bit."

After Rachel left, Emma considered what she had said and realized she believed the other woman. Try as she might, she couldn't recall a single instance where Rachel had behaved inappropriately with her father, or had given any indication she wanted him to marry her. Their brief interactions had mostly revolved around Callie, and Rachel had never acted like a scorned lover. In fact, she'd always been unfailingly kind to Emma whenever they had seen each other.

Drawing a deep breath, Emma left her bedroom. Downstairs, she was surprised to see Rachel, along with Callie's maid of honor and the wedding planner, standing outside the door to one of the first-floor guest rooms. They were speaking urgently through the closed door and from inside the room, Emma could hear the sound of muffled sobbing.

"Is that Callie?" she asked.

"She's locked herself in and won't come out," her maid of honor said. "Everyone is waiting for her! I don't know what's wrong with her."

"It's just a case of cold feet," said the wedding planner. "Perfectly normal. This happens more than people realize. If

I could just talk to her…"

"Callie, darling," Rachel called through the door. "We can't help you if you won't let us in. Damon is waiting for you. Your guests are waiting for you. Please come out."

Emma turned to the women. "Does anyone have a hairpin or a paperclip?"

"I do," the wedding planner said, and opened a large purse. She dug through it for a moment, and then pulled out two small, plastic containers. One held paperclips, and the other held an assortment of hairpins. Emma removed a hairpin and straightened it before she bent and inserted it into the keyhole opening of the doorknob. Her brother Luke had shown her this trick when she was a teenager, and needed to get into Callie's bedroom to retrieve a pilfered pair of shoes or some other article of clothing. Feeling around, she located the lock on the opposite side of the door and pushed it, and was rewarded with a small clicking sound.

Removing the hairpin, she stood up and looked at the other women. "I'll talk to her," she said, and turned the doorknob.

"Go away," Callie said when Emma stepped into the room and closed the door behind her. She made a beautifully tragic figure as she lay facedown across the bed, with her wedding gown and veil trailing onto the floor.

"You're going to crease your dress," Emma said drily. "Never mind what you're doing to your makeup."

With a startled gasp, Callie raised her head. Her face was blotchy from crying, and her freckles stood out starkly. "What are you doing here?"

"I could ask you the same thing. You have four hundred guests and a groom waiting for you. Why are you in here?"

Callie sat up and used her fingertips to blot her eyes. "I've ruined everything. Everyone is mad at me, even Damon."

"Why do you think that?" Emma asked, and came to sit on the edge of the bed. Callie did look truly miserable, and Emma felt a pang of unexpected sympathy for her.

"Because I was such a bitch to you last night, and because Holt threw Cort out this morning." She looked at Emma, her expression glum. "I'm sorry about that."

Emma sighed. "Holt didn't actually throw Cort out—he left on his own. But he did aim some pretty nasty accusations at him—none of which are true, by the way." She gave Callie a puzzled look. "Why did you feel the need to out me like that, in front of everyone?"

Callie shook her head. "I don't know. You've always been so perfect. You're the favorite daughter, the favorite sister, and everyone gets so excited when they know you're coming home for a visit. Meanwhile, I've been right here all along, but nobody even cares. They barely even notice me when I come to the ranch, and I'm here nearly every day!" She gave a mournful sniff. "It's *my* wedding, but all everyone talks about is you and Cort, and how handsome he is, and how heroic he is, and what a lovely couple you are, and how happy everyone is that you've moved on and found someone else. It's too much!"

Emma stared at her sister, dumbfounded. "Oh, Callie," she finally said. "If you only knew how wrong you are. I'm far from perfect. And I'm not the favorite daughter, not even close. Most of the time, I don't even feel like I'm part of the family. Meanwhile, you've grown up here, as much a part of this family as Holt, Evan, and Luke. Do you have any idea how much I envy you that?"

"You do?"

"Of course. All I've ever wanted is to be part of this family. It hasn't been easy, because my mother did everything she could to keep me in New York while I was growing up."

Fresh tears squeezed out of Callie's eyes. "I'm sorry, Emma. I'm the worst sister ever."

Emma gave her a rueful smile. "Pretty much."

"I think I've always been jealous of your relationship with Daddy," Callie confessed. "He always seemed so happy to see you, the way he never did with me."

"That's only because he saw you every day, and I only came to the ranch a few times each year. Trust me when I tell you that by the end of each summer, he was more than ready to send me back to New York!"

"The real reason I came to New York that summer was because my mother said sisters are important."

"They are important." Emma gave a helpless shrug. "You're the only sister I have."

"I never meant to fall in love with Damon," she said, sniffling. "I'm so sorry I hurt you."

Emma drew in a deep breath, and let it out slowly. "I don't think I was as upset about losing Damon as I was about losing you, Callie. The betrayal was what hurt the most."

Callie hung her head. "I know. I don't know if I can ever forgive myself for what I put you through. I don't know if I should marry him, because it will always be there, between us." She looked at Emma. "I don't want to lose you."

"Do you love him?"

Fresh tears leaked out of Callie's eyes. "I love him so much, Emma. I believed him when he said you two were growing apart, and that you probably would have broken up, even if we hadn't…you know. Otherwise, I wouldn't have let things go so far. But now, it's too late."

Emma's gaze sharpened on her sister. "What do you mean?"

Callie put a hand over midriff and gave Emma a meaningful look.

"What? Do you mean—?"

Callie nodded, and through her tears, she smiled. "I haven't told anyone, not even Damon. There's a part of me that wants to know he married me by choice, and not because he had to."

"Oh, Callie!" Emma said, and pulled her sister into her arms, hugging her fiercely. "Of course he's marrying you by choice. He loves you." She pulled back just far enough to look into Callie's face. "I love you, too, in spite of everything. I hope you know that." She looked meaningfully at Callie's flat stomach. "If you don't marry Damon today, either Daddy or Holt will get the shotgun out and force the issue. You know that we Claibornes are famous for our shotgun weddings. If not today, then as soon as they realize you're expecting."

Callie bit her lower lip and gave Emma a wary look. "So you don't mind?"

Emma forced herself to shrug. "Everyone's been telling me that Damon and I weren't right for each other. I guess it's because you two are. Besides…I think my heart belongs to somebody else."

"Will you see him again?"

"I'm counting on it," Emma said. "Now let's get you properly married."

⚜

EMMA SAT AT a table near the back of the enormous tent, idly twirling a champagne flute as she watched the guests dance. The wedding ceremony itself had been perfect, and there had been very few dry eyes—at least, among the female guests—when the bride and groom had each read the vows they had written. Now Emma watched as Callie danced with their father, and Damon danced with Rachel.

Half the town of Last Stand had shown up for the festivities, and Emma recognized many of the faces. Even Police Chief Shane Highwater—a local celebrity on account of his heroism—was there, dancing with a pretty woman with striking chestnut hair. Emma would have recognized the chief anywhere, since a video of him rounding up a herd of runaway longhorn cattle in the middle of downtown Last Stand had gone viral the year before.

But watching the guests only made her feel lonely, reminding her that she had no one special to dance with. Soon, she would slip away and make her way back to the house. There seemed no point in remaining. Everything she had tried so hard to avoid had happened. Here she was, alone at the wedding, and she couldn't even hold her head up and pretend she was okay because on top of everything else, all the guests knew Cort had only been her fake boyfriend. They probably thought she was still hung up on her ex.

So why had it felt so real?

"Hello, girl. Why so glum?"

Emma turned to see Minna Herdmann, the town centurion, standing next to her chair as her great-granddaughter stood close by. Minna wore a lace sheath dress in a pretty shade of robin's-egg blue, and a sparkly comb with matching crystals in her signature braid. Emma hadn't seen the older woman approach and now she started to stand up, but Minna held up a thin hand.

"No, don't stand up. If you don't mind, I'm going to sit down with you. My old bones could use the rest." She eased herself into the chair next to Emma, and turned to watch the dancing. "I remember the day your momma and daddy were married on this very spot."

"You do?"

Minna chuckled. "I'm ancient, but my memory is still sharp. Too sharp, sometimes."

"I know what you mean," Emma sympathized glumly. "There are some things that are better forgotten."

Minna turned to look at Emma, her eyes shrewd. "Like what, girl? Like love, when it leaves?"

"How did—?"

To her surprise, Minna reached out and took Emma's hands in her own. Her grip was strong, her skin warm and dry. "Love doesn't leave, girl. Not true love. If it leaves, it was never really there to begin with."

Emma wanted to groan with frustration. Just as she'd suspected, everyone thought she was still hung up on her ex.

"No, you've misunderstood," she said gently. "I'm not in love with Damon."

"I'm not talking about the groom, honey. I'm talking about the other one; the one I saw you with just yesterday."

Seeing the compassion and understanding in the older woman's eyes, Emma felt something break loose inside her. Until now, everyone had avoided the subject of Cort Channing. Nobody had asked her how she felt about him, assuming that because she hadn't known Cort for very long, that there couldn't possibly be any feelings there.

But it had been real.

"I only met him about three weeks ago," she admitted.

"I've known couples who've gotten married in less time than you've known your young man, and have gone on to stay happily married their whole lives. I know a good man when I see one." She squeezed Emma's fingers. "Love didn't leave, child. Love is waiting for you. You just need to go after it."

Emma drew in a sharp breath. How could this wizened woman possibly know of her feelings for Cort, when she was so confused about them herself?

"What if you're wrong?"

Minna chuckled, and curved one hand around Emma's

cheek. "You've been away from this town for too long, honey, or you'd know better than to even ask that question. Go on, now, because for certain, what you're missing isn't here."

Chapter Fifteen

TWO WEEKS LATER, Emma began to think Cort Channing had been a figment of her imagination. She had taken Minna's words to heart and had attempted to locate him, but her efforts had been unsuccessful. His cell phone, ruined when he'd jumped into the river to save little Lucy, still sat on her dresser. If he'd gotten a new phone in the two weeks since he'd left Riverrun, he wasn't answering it.

She tried to console herself by remembering what he'd told her—he would find her. But he'd made no effort to contact her in the past two weeks, and she was beginning to have doubts. He'd all but vanished off the face of the earth. Holt made no effort to hide the fact he thought it was all part of Cort's evil plan to hoodwink her, and women in general.

"He's probably using an alias," he said one morning. They were eating breakfast on the terrace while Emma searched the internet for any mention of Cort. "Just like his father."

"Don't antagonize her, Holt." Gus, who had been reading the local newspaper, *The Defender*, lowered his glasses and winked at Emma. "She might go back to New York, and

I'm enjoying having her home."

"Really?" Holt asked. "Even though she's done nothing but mope around for the past two weeks? If I'd known this is how she was going to act, I'd have given her and Channing my blessing. In fact, maybe I'll track him down myself and beg him to come back and take her away, just to put us all out of our misery."

Emma looked at her brother, and her voice was cool. "Do you know where he is?"

"I've made it a point not to," Holt said, his tone dry. "Because then I might feel compelled to go and kick his ass."

Emma scowled at him, still not willing to forgive him for his part in driving Cort from Riverrun. "You're going to *feel* like an ass when you realize you were wrong about him."

"That's a chance I'm willing to take."

On the table beside her laptop, Emma's phone vibrated. She glanced at it, and then silenced it. She really needed to take Cort's advice and cancel her account. She'd lost count of how many times the dating app had sent her a message, claiming to have found a perfect match for her. She wasn't interested in looking at any of the recommendations. She'd found her perfect match. Now all she needed to do was locate him.

Following the wedding, Emma had called her mother to tell her she was staying in Last Stand indefinitely. Until she knew where Cort had gone, she couldn't go back to New York. Her mother had threatened to fire her from her job at the gallery, but Emma had been firm, insisting it was time she took charge of her own career. She no longer wanted to sell other people's paintings. She wanted to sell her own work. In fact, one of Callie's bridesmaids had seen the poppy painting she'd given to Callie for her wedding, and had asked if Emma could do something similar for her. It was a start, anyway.

Callie and Damon had returned from their honeymoon four days earlier, and had left again almost immediately for a three-week book tour to promote Damon's latest release. Now here it was, the Fourth of July, and the entire town was anticipating the parade that would kick off the annual rodeo over at the fairgrounds. Emma had decided to skip the opening festivities, and go straight to the bull riding event, just in case Cort decided to show.

"Holt," she said now, "if you really want to make amends, why don't you just tell me where Cort is? I know you know."

"I'm not letting you make a damned fool of yourself over him," Holt said, his blue eyes intense. "You deserve better."

"Than what? A man who's trying to make an honest living and reclaim what should have been his in the first place? There's no proof that he's any of the things you accused him of. In fact, if he ever comes back here, you'll owe him an apology."

"If he ever comes back here, he'll get more than an apology; he'll get my boot in his—"

"Excuse me, Señor Claiborne?"

Rosa-Maria stood in the doorway that led from the kitchen. She looked upset, which was unlike her. Emma had only ever known her to be a calm and happy presence in the

Claiborne household. She rarely lost her temper or became flustered. If Emma didn't know better, she'd think Rosa-Maria was actually annoyed.

"Yes, Rosa-Maria?" Gus asked.

"There is a woman here to see Emmaline."

"Me?" Emma asked in surprise.

"I decided if you really are serious about staying in Texas and selling your work, you'll need a gallery showing," declared Natalie Germaine as she strode past Rosa-Maria and onto the terrace. "I happen to have a connection here in Last Stand, and she's agreed to look at your work."

Gus shot to his feet so fast, he nearly knocked his chair over, while Emma and Holt stared at her, open-mouthed. Natalie looked as if she'd just stepped off the pages of *Vogue* magazine, in a matching navy jacket and pencil skirt edged with white piping, paired with heels and a white wide-brimmed hat. Now she pulled her sunglasses off and swept them all with a look that might have been aloof had Emma not known it was an act.

Her mother was terrified. Only Emma knew what it had cost her to come back to Last Stand.

"Hello, Gus," Natalie said. "You look good, but you should cut back on the chalupas; you've gained weight." Her gaze slid to Holt, and Emma saw her expression soften. "Hello, Holt. You're as handsome as ever. How are you?"

Holt stood up and came around the table to enfold Natalie in an embrace. "Hello, Nan," he said gruffly, using the nickname he'd given her when he was a boy and she'd been his stepmother, however briefly. "It's good to see you.

Thanks for the birthday gift you sent, by the way."

When he released her and stepped back, Emma could see her mother's eyes were moist. She laughed, and used her fingertips to swipe away the tears. "Oh, dear, I wasn't expecting to become emotional, but it really is good to see you. Both of you."

Recalling his manners, Gus walked toward her and gave her a brief hug. "This really is a nice surprise, Natalie. Come sit down."

Behind her, Rosa-Maria lifted her chin before she turned and stalked back into the house.

"I won't stay," Natalie said, but accepted the chair Gus held out for her. "I only came to see how Emma is managing. How are you doing, darling?"

Leaning over, Emma kissed her mother's cheek. "I'm glad you came, Mom. What did you say about a gallery showing?"

Natalie smiled. "I brought all your paintings with me; it cost a fortune, but I expect you'll be able to repay me when you sell them. A friend of mine runs the art gallery downtown, and she wants to do a showing." She innocently rounded her eyes as both Gus and Emma stared at her in disbelief. "What? You don't think I burned *all* my bridges when I left Texas, do you?"

Emma laughed and hugged her mother. "Mom, you are really something, do you know that? *Thank you.*"

"You're welcome. And what have you heard about your young man? Has he absconded with your fortune? Is he living under an assumed name with some other unsuspecting victim?"

"Oh, for Pete's sake," Emma exclaimed. "Have you been talking with Holt?"

"No, but I did hire someone to check on him—"

"You know where he is!" Emma exclaimed, and shot a triumphant look at her brother.

"Nan, no!" Holt said at the same time. "Don't say another word."

"Go ahead and tell her," said Gus.

"Oh, dear," Natalie murmured. "I don't want to cause any trouble, but he's actually here, in Last Stand. He's competing in the bull riding event this afternoon."

"Oh, Mom, thank you!" Emma cried, and hugged her mother again before surging to her feet. "I have to get ready! What will I wear? What time is he riding? Oh my God, he's *here*!"

"Relax, darlin'," Gus said, smiling. "We have hours yet before his event."

Emma pressed her hands against her stomach in an effort to quell the sudden butterflies that gathered and swirled there. "I'm so nervous. What if he's changed his mind?"

Holt made a scoffing sound. "I don't believe this."

"Careful, son," Gus said. "You liked him well enough before you poked around in his background. If things aren't what you think they are, you may yet get to apologize to him."

Natalie leaned toward Holt and lowered her voice to a conspiratorial stage whisper. "You may want to start practicing. Or maybe call the bakery and see if you can order a big helping of humble pie."

"Honestly," Holt said, looking at Emma, "I'd like nothing better. I'm a little weary of getting the cold shoulder in my own home."

"Well," Natalie said, "I should get going. I'm staying at the bed-and-breakfast downtown through the middle of next week. Emma, your paintings are at the gallery. We can set up a time to talk with the owner once she's had a chance to view them all." She paused and gave Emma a thorough scrutiny. "You were right not to want to bring those outfits from New York. Texas suits you. Enjoy the rodeo."

"Will you come with us?" Emma asked.

"No, darling." She smiled. "I've had my last stand. Now it's your turn."

✂

THE RODEO TOOK place in an historic arena that had hosted the annual Fourth of July event since the turn of the century. By the time Emma, Holt, Evan, and Gus arrived, the stands were nearly full, and the crowd was cheering its approval for the barrel-racing event.

The smell of animals, manure, and fresh sawdust contrasted with the tantalizing aromas of funnel cakes, grilled bratwurst, and kettle corn, bringing Emma right back to her childhood when she had attended the rodeo with her father and brothers. Patriotic flags had been draped around the arena in celebration of the day, and the announcer kept up a colorful commentary over the loudspeakers, keeping the audience entertained as each contestant entered the arena.

They sat in the bleacher stands near the bull chutes, and Emma stood up, straining to get a look at the riders. But with their hats, protective vests, and colorful chaps, they all looked unfamiliar to her.

"I can't tell if he's here," she complained to no one in particular. "Maybe I should go down and walk through the pens."

"You should stay here," Evan suggested. "The bull riding event is next, and his name is in the program. You'll see him soon enough."

"I could go down there and wish him luck," she said.

"You'll distract him, more likely," Evan replied, giving her a wink. "You don't want to be the reason he has a wreck in the arena."

Evan was right. Reluctantly, Emma sat down again and tried to focus on the barrel racing. She wore the boots and hat that Cort had chosen for her, along with a pair of shorts and a sleeveless cotton top in a pretty shade of pink. She knew that following the rodeo, there would be music, dancing, and fireworks, and she wanted to look nice. When they finally announced the bull riding event, Emma thought she would crawl out of her skin with anxiety and anticipation. As it was, they first had to sit through the calf riding, and then the junior bull riding, where local teenagers tried their best to stay seated on specially bred miniature bulls.

Finally, former PBR star Trent Campbell announced the bull riding event. He introduced the riders, and Emma got her first glimpse of Cort in two weeks. He wore a black hat, and his protective vest was covered in sponsor logos and patches. His chaps were black as well, heavily tooled in red, and sported long, red fringe.

Emma had never seen anyone look as masculine or sexy as he did, standing there with his head bowed, feet planted apart, and hands crossed as he listened to Trent make the introductions. Then they made their way to the bull chutes, directly below where Emma and her family sat.

"I can see him mounting his bull," she said to Holt, pointing to the pen where Cort was lowering himself onto the back of a white bull.

"He drew Bad to the Bone," Evan replied, referring to the bull's name.

"Is he a good bull?" Emma asked.

"He's a good one for racking up points," Holt replied, "but bad if you're not an experienced rider."

"Cort will do fine," Emma said, more to convince herself than her brother. "I've seen him ride; he's very good."

There were ten riders, and Cort was number three. They watched as the first was thrown to the ground within five seconds. The second managed to stay seated for the full eight seconds, but his score was just mediocre since his bull was more of a runner than a bucker. Finally, they announced Cort's name.

Emma watched as they pulled the gate open, and bull and rider exploded into the arena in a frenzy of flying sawdust and mud. Cort kept one arm up and away from his body, jerking with each buck and kick of the animal beneath him, red fringe flying dramatically as the bull spun and twisted. Then the buzzer sounded, and Cort dismounted, landing heavily in the sawdust, to the delighted cheers of the crowd. But the bull was still spinning, and as Cort tried to scramble to safety, the animal's front feet came down squarely on top of him, pushing him back to the ground.

Emma and the crowd gave a collective gasp, and she surged to her feet as the bullfighters moved in to distract the bull and lead him away. Cort was still on the ground and, as she watched, several cowboys ran into the arena and bent over him.

"I can't see!" Emma cried. "What's happened to him? Is he hurt? I need to go down there!"

But her father stopped her with one hand on her arm. "You stay here, darlin'. You'll only be in the way."

Seeing his grave expression, she knew it must be bad. He was trying to protect her from seeing Cort injured, or worse. The bull riding community had lost a rider earlier that year after he'd been stomped on by a bull, and now dread settled into Emma's heart, cold and heavy and insistent.

She couldn't lose Cort.

"I'm going down there," she said, and her father withdrew his hand.

"We'll all go," Holt said.

But by the time they reached the ground level of the arena and the pens where the bulls were kept, Cort was being rolled on a stretcher toward a waiting ambulance. Emma could barely see him, surrounded as he was by medical personnel and arena staff, but he looked to be sitting up. Then they lifted his stretcher into the back of the ambulance, and closed the doors.

"They'll take him to Jameson Hospital," Gus said. "Holt, you drive."

"If you want to get there this week, I'll drive," said Evan, giving his brother a friendly punch on the shoulder.

Evan was a volunteer firefighter in Last Stand, and frequently had to race to the fire station to respond to an emergency. Holt, on the other hand, was all about safety and following the law. He'd no doubt drive well below the speed limit and come to a complete stop at every intersection on the way to the hospital. Emma was grateful Holt didn't argue, and soon they were in Holt's pickup truck and roaring through the nearly deserted roads toward the hospital.

Inside the emergency room, Gus spoke with the nurse on duty at the triage center, and learned Cort had been taken in for X-rays. They spoke quietly for several minutes before he rejoined Emma and her brothers in the waiting area.

"He was conscious and alert when they brought him in," he said. "The bull stepped on his shoulder, and they suspect he has a broken collarbone and arm, but they're running tests now to be certain there's no other damage."

Emma sagged against Holt, overwhelmed with the force of her relief. "Oh, thank goodness. When can we see him?"

"It might be a while," Evan said. "If you're determined to stay, you might as well make yourself comfortable."

"You don't have to stay," Emma replied, "but I'm not leaving."

"Then we'll stay with you," Holt said. "It's only right, especially if he's not the villain we've made him out to be."

"Not *we*," Emma corrected him. "*You*. I never had any doubts."

While the Claiborne men took seats in the waiting area, Emma paced restlessly, continually looking down the length of the long corridor toward the imaging department, as if she could will Cort into sight. She called her mother and explained what had happened, and soon Natalie arrived at the hospital to lend her support. Two hours later, there was still no sign of Cort, and no word from the hospital staff on his condition.

"He's okay, don't you worry," Natalie said, putting her arms around Emma. "Bull riders are a tough breed, you'll see."

"Mom," Emma said, leaning back in her mother's arms. "Do you really know something about Cort's past that we don't know?"

"When you said you weren't returning to New York because of this man, I absolutely did some checking. You're a woman with a trust fund, darling, and a wealthy father. Do you think I'd let you run off with just anybody?"

"Where has he been for two weeks, and what did you learn?"

Natalie glanced over Emma's shoulder, and smiled. "Maybe you should ask him yourself."

Whirling around, Emma saw Cort being pushed toward them in a wheelchair. He wore a hospital johnny over his jeans and boots, and a cast encased his left arm, which had been secured tightly to his body in a blue fabric sling. A plastic bag with his personal belongings sat on his lap. Seeing

Emma, he motioned for the orderly to stop the wheelchair. Standing, he began to walk toward Emma, and even from a distance she could see the glow in his green eyes, and the grin on his face.

"Oh, Cort," she breathed, and began walking swiftly toward him, stopping only when she was a foot away. Her gaze went to his arm and emotion made her voice unsteady. "I want so badly to hug you."

"Honey, that's why God gave me two arms—so when one gets busted, I can still hold you with the other. Come here." The deep, smoky quality of his voice still had the ability to raise delicious goosebumps on her skin, and she willingly went into his embrace, careful of his arm as she nuzzled her face into the base of his throat and breathed him in.

"I've missed you so much," she said, her voice trembling.

"God, I've missed you too," he said as he bent his head and kissed her long and hard.

"Where have you been all this time?" she asked when she could speak again.

"I had some stuff I needed to take care of before I came back to Last Stand."

"Are you okay?"

"Broken collarbone, and my arm's busted, but I'll mend," he said. "Of course, I won't be riding in any events for at least three to four months, so I doubt I'll be invited to Las Vegas."

He sounded oddly cheerful for a man who had counted on winning the prize money at the invitational, and had now lost that opportunity.

Gus stepped forward and shook Cort's hand. "Good to see you in one piece, son. That was a helluva ride."

"And a helluva dismount," Evan said, also shaking Cort's hand. "Glad it wasn't any worse."

"Let's get you back to Riverrun and make you comfortable," Gus suggested.

"They loaded me up pretty good with painkillers, so I'm actually feeling very comfortable. If you don't mind, I have a room at the B and B on Bluebonnet Lane. I've imposed on your hospitality enough, so I'll stay there tonight."

Gus looked at Emma and raised an eyebrow. "I know, you don't have to tell me twice—you're a couple and you'll stay together."

"Thank you, Daddy." Emma barely heard him, arrested by the expression in Cort's eyes as he looked at her.

"I'll drive them into town," Natalie offered. "But first, don't you think you should tell them what happened, Cort?" She gave Holt an apologetic smile. "We ran into each other last night at the B and B as he was checking in. You can imagine my surprise when I realized who he was. He wanted to drive straight out to the ranch, but I persuaded him to have dinner with me, instead, and he told me everything. So I had insider knowledge when I came by the house earlier, but the story is his to tell, not mine."

Cort handed Emma the plastic bag with his personal effects inside. "Emma, there's an envelope in here somewhere. Would you mind fishing it out for me?"

Emma found the envelope and opened it, withdrawing

two letters. One had the official letterhead of a Texas law firm. The second letter looked personal.

"You had this with you when you rode that bull this afternoon?" she asked.

"That letter hasn't left my sight since I received it last week, and my intention was to head straight to the ranch after the rodeo and share it with you."

"Maybe this should wait until tomorrow," Holt said. "You should get some rest, Channing."

"No, you'll want to hear this. It's important, in light of our last conversation," Cort said.

Holt had the grace to look embarrassed. "I was out of line. Whatever your father did or didn't do is no reflection on you or your character. I know that. I hope you'll accept my apology."

"You were just looking out for your sister," Cort said. "No apology necessary,"

Reaching out with his good hand, he shook Holt's hand.

Natalie smiled her approval. "Now that we're all friends again, go ahead and tell them, Cort."

"Yes, ma'am. You already know that my birth father stole a sizable amount of cash and three canisters of bull seed from my granddad," Cort said. "The petty cash was one thing, but the bull seed was valued at over a quarter of a million dollars. My granddad insisted my father stole those canisters, but the police were never able to prove anything. Worse, the insurance wouldn't cover the theft because the breeding barn had been left unlocked. The financial loss was devastating."

He paused and took hold of Emma's hand. "My mother

was consumed with guilt over what my father had done, and was determined to track Roy Channing down and make him return the bull seed, or tell her where she could find it. She blamed herself for bringing Roy into the family, for trusting him. It took her nearly two years, but she finally tracked him to Nevada. He was married to another woman and living under an alias."

"Did he have the bull seed?" Emma asked. She could only imagine what his mother had endured, knowing the man she loved had betrayed her.

"If he did, he didn't tell her. Or if he told her, she never had the chance to pass that information along to my grand-dad. She was killed in a head-on collision driving back to Texas. I was four years old." Cort was silent for a moment, lost in contemplation. "My granddad made me feel guilty for what my dad had done my whole life. He never, ever, cut me a break. Hell, he all but blamed me for my own mother's death."

"None of that was your fault, son," Gus said. "You were a child. What happened to your father?"

Cort shook his head. "I have no idea. After my mother died, my granddad dropped all the charges against him, but he never let me forget that my father was a bigamist and a thief. I grew up despising Roy Channing, and feeling guilty as hell because I was a constant reminder to my grandfather of everything he had lost. I never tried to find him, and he sure as hell never came around looking for a relationship with me."

"So what's in that letter?" Holt asked, indicating the two

documents in Cort's hands.

Cort handed one of the letters to Holt. "My granddad's confession."

Emma frowned. "For what?"

"He knew all along that Roy was trying to convince my mother to steal money. Hell, Granddad made it easy for him. He withdrew most of the cash from the safe, and left just enough to satisfy Roy and ensure he took off. But Roy Channing never stole those canisters of bull seed."

"How do you know?" asked Gus.

Holt had finished reading the letter, and now he handed it back to Cort.

"Because my granddad says here that he stole the canisters himself," Cort said. "He wanted to make it look as if Roy had stolen the bull seed, in order to convince my mother that she had married a no-good loser. I think he believed she would continue to champion Roy if he'd only taken the money, but if my grandfather could convince her he'd taken the bull seed, too, and put the ranch in jeopardy, she would finally divorce him. In reality, he stored the canisters at a fertilization center in Oklahoma, under a false name, with instructions to keep the seed viable until he returned to claim it. My guess is he was going to do that as soon as my mother divorced Roy Channing. Only she never got the chance."

"Oh my God," Emma breathed. "She tracked Roy down in order to get the canisters back, because she felt so guilty about your granddad's financial loss."

Cort nodded. "The loss was real. He still had other canisters of bull seed, but they were from lesser bulls, and they couldn't command the same money or prestige as the seed that had gone missing. Not even close. My granddad knew he couldn't retrieve the three missing canisters from the storage facility, because he'd told everyone they'd been stolen. It would have looked pretty suspicious if they just magically turned up one day. He'd been counting on the insurance settlement to pay him for the loss, but they refused to pay out because the breeding barn had been left unlocked. They claimed negligence on his part. He really was in financial distress."

"And then his daughter was killed, trying to correct what essentially was his mess," Holt said.

"Yes. After her death, he was so consumed with grief and guilt over his part in the deception that he could never bring himself to reclaim those canisters of bull seed. They've been sitting in that fertilization center for more than two decades."

There was a moment of stunned silence, as each of them absorbed what Cort had revealed. As she watched him relate the story so matter-of-factly, Emma's heart broke for him. His entire life he'd wanted nothing more than his granddad's approval, and the old man had denied him that, even knowing that what he'd done had been almost as bad as what Roy Channing had done.

"So what are you going to do?" Emma asked.

"My granddad went to the center about five years ago and legally transferred ownership of the bull seed to me. So when the bank came in and took the ranch, those canisters were no longer part of the estate. They belong to me, and this letter from the attorney says it's all legal."

"And the bull seed is still good?" Emma asked. "After all this time?"

"That's what I asked," said Natalie with a smirk. "Why anyone would want twenty-five-year-old sperm is beyond me."

"There is no expiration date on frozen semen," Holt assured them. "As long as the seed is properly maintained in a liquid nitrogen storage tank, the life span is believed to be unlimited. I know cases where frozen semen resulted in pregnancies decades after it had been stored."

"Oh, Cort," Emma said. "I'm so happy for you. After all these years, though...I wonder why he couldn't have told you this when he was alive?"

"I think he was too ashamed, both by his part in the scheme and by the way he treated me all my life. But at least now I can understand why he treated me so badly. Somehow, by directing all his anger and unhappiness toward me, he didn't need to deal with his own grief over losing his daughter." He looked at Emma. "But old age and impending death have a way of making you see what's really important. He gave this letter to his lawyer about five years ago with instructions to give it to me on the first anniversary of his death."

"I'm just sorry he thought he needed to wait until after he was gone to settle things," Emma replied. "What will you do now?"

"If I can't buy back Granddad's property, I'll find another piece of land somewhere and look for a partner who understands the intricacies of bull breeding." He looked pointedly at Holt. "Maybe you know of someone, Holt?"

Emma might have laughed at the comical expression of surprise on Holt's face, if she hadn't known how serious the topic was.

"Christ, what kind of drugs did they give you?" Evan asked, laughing. "Don't make any promises or important decisions right now, that's my advice."

"Evan's right. Let's talk in a few days, when you're not feeling the effects of the medication they've pumped into you," Holt finally replied. "But I'm looking forward to the discussion."

"And now, I think we should let you get some rest," Gus interjected.

Cort grimaced. "I think you're right. Those painkillers are starting to wear off."

"I'm going back to the B and B," Natalie said. "Let me drive you."

As Cort put his good arm around her, Emma saw the glint in his eyes and suspected he had no intention of sleeping. Her heartbeat quickened with anticipation.

He was back, and she was exactly where she belonged—in his arms.

Chapter Sixteen

C ORT RESTED AGAINST the bed pillows that Emma had stacked against the headboard, watching her as she moved around the room at the B and B. He had slept for several hours while she returned to the ranch and packed a bag for herself. She'd picked up takeout from Hilde's Haus, the local diner, and had returned to the B and B just as Cort was waking up.

"I could use a shower," he said now, his voice velvet-rough with sleep.

He looked like a big, sleepy cat with his slumberous green eyes, and his short hair sticking up in places. He was bare-chested, and his skin gleamed bronze against the creamy white bed linens, except for where a dark bruise had begun to bloom across his shoulder.

Emma had pulled the drapes closed to keep the afternoon sun out of the room. The air-conditioning stirred the fabric and wafted cool air through the room.

She looked doubtfully at his arm, which was still secured tightly against his ribs with the sling. "Are you able to get your cast wet?"

Cort glanced at the black cast that extended from his fingers, and up over his elbow. "It's fiberglass, so it should be okay." He raised his eyes to hers, and Emma caught her breath at the blatant invitation she saw there. "I'll probably need help, though. Feel like gettin' wet, honey?"

Emma's knees went a little weak, and she struggled to remember that he'd been injured by a bull only hours earlier. "Are you sure you're up for it?"

In answer, Cort pushed back the bedcovers and swung his feet to the floor. He wore only a pair of boxer briefs, and beneath the stretchy material, he was already hard. All the saliva in Emma's mouth evaporated as he stood. She'd seen him in his boxers before, but the lighting had been too muted for her to fully appreciate just how sleek and masculine he really was.

"Come here," he said to her, and held out his good arm.

Emma stepped into his embrace, keeping her hands lightly on his waist as she leaned up to kiss him.

"You're not going to hurt me," he whispered. "I've been in worse wrecks. This is nothing."

He slanted his mouth over hers, kissing her softly at first, until Emma sighed into his mouth and pressed closer, letting one hand drift down to his boxers and the rigid rise of his erection. Cort groaned and deepened the kiss, tangling his tongue with hers. Emboldened, Emma slid her hand inside the stretchy waistband and gripped the hard, silken length. Cort's breathing quickened as Emma stroked him, tentatively at first, and then with more confidence.

"Darlin'," he finally rasped, "this is going to be over before it's begun if you don't quit that now."

But Emma had no intention of stopping. She felt as if she'd been waiting her whole life for Cort Channing. Despite having only known him for a short time, she was more connected to him than she'd ever been to Damon. She'd thought she could never fall in love with a cowboy, and now she knew she would never stop loving this one.

Stepping out of his embrace, she sat down on the edge of the bed and pulled her boots off, tossing them aside before she quickly removed her shirt and shorts. Aware of Cort watching her, she reached behind her back and unfastened her bra, letting it drop to the floor before she shimmied out of her panties. Cort had gone still as he watched her, hectic color riding high on his chiseled cheekbones.

"Christ, honey, you're beautiful," he breathed. "I don't think I could ever get tired of seeing you like this."

"Make love to me, Cort," she pleaded. "This time, all the way."

Gripping him by the hips, she drew him close and began pressing kisses against his body, starting at his chest and working her way down his torso, over the hard muscles of his stomach, until she reached his boxers. Sliding both hands into the waistband, she tugged them down until his erection sprang free. Cort stepped out of the boxers and didn't resist as Emma drew him toward the bed. Sitting on the edge of the mattress, she ran her hands along his length, admiring the heft and strength in her hands. When she rubbed her thumb over the blunted head, she was rewarded with a slick of moisture.

Cort groaned, and moved one hand to Emma's head,

lightly sifting his fingers through her hair. Bending forward, Emma took him into her mouth, tasting him lightly at first, and then deeper, feeling his entire body go taut. She drew on him, and cupped him from beneath, stroking his heated skin and relishing his hard length. Helplessly, he thrust forward and Emma took him deeper, one hand going to his backside to cup a hard-muscled buttock. She felt him swell even more, and knew he was close. But he pulled away, his breathing quick and hard. Emma looked up at him through her lashes. His eyes were drowsy with pleasure, his face flushed.

"Good?" she asked softly.

"If it was any better, I'd be dead," he said, his voice roughened with desire.

"Come here," Emma said, and lay back across the bed, extending her arms to pull Cort into the splayed opening of her legs. "This way you won't have to strain your shoulder."

"Are you sure, honey?" His eyes were riveted on her.

"Surer than I've been of anything in a long time."

"I don't know if I can go gently," he said. "I want you too much. I've wanted you since the first time I saw your picture on that damned dating app."

"Really?"

"Honest to God. When Rhys showed me your profile, I was a goner. If he had decided to go through with the date, I think I would have had to hurt him. I knew then you were meant to be mine."

"Oh, Cort," she breathed, her heart near to bursting with emotion. "Someday you're going to tell me what happened to Rhys."

"I'll tell you now. The night he was supposed to meet you, a woman showed up on his doorstep and told him she was pregnant with his baby."

"An ex-girlfriend?"

"I'm not sure they were ever officially a couple, but he's decided to try to make it work."

"Well, you don't have to worry about that with me." Emma gripped him in her hand and drew him closer, until she felt the broad tip nudging at her center. "I'm on the pill," she said softly, "so we don't need a condom, unless you want one."

Cort swallowed hard. "I've never ridden bareback."

"Never?"

"Never wanted to take the chance."

"Take a chance with me, Cort," Emma said. "Love me."

Trapping her gaze with his own, Cort surged forward, sliding into her in two long, powerful thrusts. Emma hadn't been with anyone in nearly two years, and Cort wasn't a small man. The sensation of being stretched and filled overwhelmed her. Lifting her hips, she took him deeper, digging her heels into the edge of the mattress as Cort started a slow, steady rhythm, coaxing a response from her body.

"You're snug," he managed to gasp, moving his hips against hers in a way that caused pleasure to gather and swirl.

Emma tightened her muscles, clenching around the hard length inside her, loving how Cort groaned in response. His eyes glowed as he reached down and pressed his thumb against her sensitized flesh, circling the wet nub until Emma was helpless to prevent her soft cries of pleasure.

"That's it, honey," he said, pumping into her. "Come for me."

He thrust faster now, harder, his fingers working magic on her body until the spasms began, rolling over her in hard waves as she contracted around him. She watched Cort's face as he found his own release, and even then he didn't stop, coaxing every last shudder from her spent body.

Afterward, he eased himself onto the bed beside her, using pillows to support his shoulder and arm, and nestling her against his good side. Emma traced an invisible map across his chest and abdomen, her cheek resting on his chest as she listened to the hard thump of his heart beneath her ear.

"What happens now?" she asked, tipping her face up to look at him.

"Now we spend the rest of the weekend doing what we just did," he said, laughing softly. "Over and over again. I don't think a lifetime is going to be enough time for me to get my fill of you."

Emma's heart skipped a beat. "Is that what you want? A lifetime?"

Cort swallowed hard and she heard his heartbeat quicken. "I'm not good at feelings, honey, but I know I want to be with you, for however long you want to put up with me. If it's a lifetime, so much the better."

"What about your bull riding?"

Cort's expression was serious as he searched her face. "I'm not sure bull riding is in my future anymore. I meant what I said when I told Holt I'd be looking for a partner. If he's interested, I'd count myself lucky to work with him.

With his knowledge, and my granddad's seed stock, I think we can build up a reputable business raising bucking bulls."

"Do you still want to buy your granddad's ranch?"

Cort hesitated. "I thought I'd talk to Holt about that. If he wants it, I won't stand in his way. We can add the rest of my granddad's seed stock to our business, and maybe sell off the land separately. I think I'll take your father's advice and look for some land here in Last Stand."

"You've really given this some thought," Emma said.

"Honey, since you came into my life, I've thought of nothing else." He was quiet for a moment. "I know you and your sister have your issues, but she's still your family. I know you've felt like you don't belong here, like you're an outsider, but I've seen the way your family treats you. They love you, Emmaline. I never had anything like what you have here, and it's not something you just turn your back on."

"I realize that now," Emma said. "Callie and I settled our differences on her wedding day. Seems she was feeling as much of an outsider as I was. Silly, really, all that time wasted. My mother brought all my paintings from New York with her. I have an appointment with a gallery here in Last Stand next week. What would you think if I took up painting full-time?"

"I think that's a great idea. You deserve a fresh start," Cort said. "Will you stay here in Last Stand with me, Emmaline Claiborne?"

Raising herself on one elbow, Emma searched his face. Everything she felt for him, she saw reflected in his eyes. "I've fallen in love with you, Cort Channing. When I opened that account on the dating app, I never in a million years expected to find you. I had always told myself I would never, ever fall for a cowboy."

As if on cue, Emma's cell phone vibrated on the nightstand beside the bed. She didn't even bother picking it up, knowing exactly what it was.

"Someone trying to reach you?" Cort asked.

Emma grimaced. "No. It's that dating app I joined. I still haven't closed my account, and I've been getting endless notifications that they've found me a perfect match."

"Let's take a look," Cort suggested. He held out his hand.

"Cort, I have no interest in any of their recommendations. In case you haven't noticed, I'm already involved with someone."

Cort's expression warmed as he looked at her. "Yes, you are. But I'm curious. Hand it over."

With a soft groan, Emma picked up her phone and pulled up the dating app. She punched in her password and handed the device to Cort. "I haven't even been on the app since I met you," she said. "I have no idea how many recommended 'matches' they've found."

"Well, let's see," he murmured softly as he opened the app. "It says they've found a match who is compatible with you in every way." Cort gave a soft grunt. "Hmm. He's not bad looking."

Emma refused to be baited. "I'm not interested."

"He's financially secure and looking for a long-term, permanent relationship. Says he prefers artistic types."

"Still don't care, and still not looking," Emma replied.

"Says he wants to have long, slow sex with you, in every position there is, including cowgirl. Says he can make you forget your own name."

"*What?*" Emma snatched the phone from him, outraged. "Let me see that!"

She looked at the image on the phone, and then turned to Cort in shock. "Cort Channing, this is a picture of *you!*" She scanned the description beneath the photo. "And there's absolutely no mention of sex here."

Cort chuckled. "But it made you look, didn't it?"

"When did you create an account?" she asked, still reeling from the knowledge that Cort had not only opened an account, but had managed to put himself at the top of the list for a qualified match.

"The day I met you, in Manhattan," he admitted. "I didn't want you to date anyone else."

"My phone kept sending me notifications, but I never looked at any of them."

"Think of what you might have missed," he teased, but his eyes were serious as he searched her face. "The only question is, what are you going to do now?"

Leaning down, Emma pressed a lingering kiss against his luscious mouth. "What do you think?" she asked. "I'm going to swipe right for a cowboy, now and always."

"As long as it's this cowboy," Cort said, sliding his hand to the back of her scalp, and holding her still. "I think it's a perfect match."

The End

If you enjoyed this book, please leave a review at your favorite online retailer! Even if it's just a sentence or two it makes all the difference.

Thanks for reading *Swipe Right for a Cowboy* by Karen Foley!

Discover your next romance at TulePublishing.com.

TULE
PUBLISHING

If you enjoyed *Swipe Right for a Cowboy,*
you'll love the next books in….

The Riverrun Ranch series

Book 1: *Swipe Right for a Cowboy*

Book 2: *Coming May 2020!*

Book 3: *Coming June 2020!*

Available now at your favorite online retailer!

More books by Karen Foley

The Glacier Creek series

Book 1: *A Hot Montana Summer*

Book 2: *The Firefighter's Slow Burn*

Book 3: *A Soldier's Homecoming*

Available now at your favorite online retailer!

About the Author

Karen Foley admits to being an incurable romantic. When she's not working for the Department of Defense, she loves writing sexy stories about alpha heroes and strong heroines. Karen lives in New England with her husband, two daughters, and a houseful of pets.

Thank you for reading

Swipe Right for a Cowboy

If you enjoyed this book, you can find more from all our great authors at TulePublishing.com, or from your favorite online retailer.

TULE
PUBLISHING

Made in the USA
Monee, IL
28 July 2021

74474797R00150